A Field of Wild Flowers

A Field of Wild Flowers

❦

DeLeon DeMicoli

Writer's Showcase
San Jose New York Lincoln Shanghai

A Field of Wild Flowers

All Rights Reserved © 2002 by DeLeon DeMicoli

No part of this book may be reproduced or transmitted in any form or by any means, graphic, electronic, or mechanical, including photocopying, recording, taping, or by any information storage retrieval system, without the permission in writing from the publisher.

Writer's Showcase
an imprint of iUniverse, Inc.

For information address:
iUniverse, Inc.
5220 S. 16th St., Suite 200
Lincoln, NE 68512
www.iuniverse.com

Any resemblance to actual people and events is purely coincidental.
This is a work of fiction.

ISBN: 0-595-23438-0

Printed in the United States of America

CHAPTER 1

❁

I am ten years old, walking down the sidewalk on my way to school.
My lips are dry.
My nose hairs are stuck to the edge of my nostrils.
The temperature is so cold I can see my breath turn into icicles, they stop in mid air and drop to the ground shattering beneath my feet.

I am ten years old, walking along the sidewalk next to a street.
I see the exhaust smoke of cars as they drive past a blinking yellow light signal.
The exhaust twirls in circles until it blends in with the air.
The yellow light reminds me of the sun, the only color in this muted gray landscape.

I am ten years old, walking along the black pavement on my way to school.
Ahead I see some children playing in front of their classroom door.
Girls are huddled together to keep warm.
Boys are running in circles.

I am ten years old, walking along the black pavement that forks off into two directions.
The fork to the left leads through the playground amongst the children.
The fork to the right journeys through the outer perimeter of the playground into a neighborhood I've never walked along.

I am ten years old, and I'm walking to the right.
I am scared of what to expect.
I am scared about what I might figure out.
I want to play like the others and run around chasing balls.
But the temptation of wandering in another direction has me curious.

The path leads me to a creek
The Creek—The one that divides my apartment complex and a neighborhood I've never walked through until now.
All I can think is *I've never lived in a house.*

I am ten years old and I jump across the creek back to my surroundings.
When my feet hit the ground I become sixteen, standing at a bus station.
I look around at the people next to me; a man is suited up in a charcoal three-piece suit wearing a top hat. He's reading the paper.
A lady is sitting at the bench staring out to the field on the opposite side of the tracks.
A train pulls up, but with no sound.
I ask myself out loud if I'm going deaf. "Can you hear me?"

I am sixteen years old and boarding the train without a ticket.
Beep.
I find a seat next to an old man who just looks out his window,

watching the tall grass from the field sway back and forth.
I am asking him if he knows where this train is going.
Beep.
He turns his head my way.
Beep.
"Do you know what I'm doing here?"
Beep. Beep.
He begins to speak, but I don't hear what's coming outta his mouth; all I see are his lips moving.
Beep. Beep. Beep.

I am sixteen years old sitting next to an old man on a train that begins to move.
I don't . *Beep.* Know. *Beep.* Where. *Beep.* I'm going...

I just woke up.

Every weekday morning is like a rainy gray Sunday. I feel dazed, disfigured, crooked at the hellish sound of my alarm clock.

I hate feeling like this early in the morning. The birds from the other side of the window sill are flying and chirping, while I lay in bed wishing I was a bird hunter, killing anything that takes me away from my dreams. A couple of seconds ago it was still nighttime for me, when my mind digs itself zombie-like out of its coffin to play, scare, and enlighten my subconscious, but those goddamn birds ruined it all, like they do every bright morning. However, it's not all their fault. The morning car alarm clock creep-beeps into the REMs of my subconscious, like in those old 70's sci-fi movies, where the hero dressed in tight silver disco polyester is placed in a rubber white room and tortured to the sharp high-pitched sounds that blow out his eardrums. Isn't that the idea—to send electricity through the wires, and then, amplified by a channel of psychotic beeps, to send sound bombs around the room and into the eardrums of the victim?

Well, that's how my brain explodes into a fury of wakefulness, making my eyes roll up and down behind the shades of my eyelids until they are dark red and open and awake.

"Noooo. Not yet, just a little more time," I yell, placing the pillow over my head and screaming for silence. And I know silence is only a push away, but I'm too lazy to close the window.

This tussle goes on until I realize that the beep-beep hasn't stopped. It continues more insistently, more monotonously to demand, from across the room, that I wake up for a good cause. I have school today, kinda'.

I lie on my stomach, slipping my left hand out from under the covers out onto the cool room morning air, hitting the off button on my alarm clock, and then lying still, waiting for that burst of energy to roll me out and into the bathroom. Mom begins pounding on my door, which seems to bend towards me at least a foot with each blow and then return to me unscathed just like in the cartoons.

I'm still not moving.

"Sol, get the hell up. I'm not driving your butt to school today, I'm runnin' late myself."

"All right, I'm up," I yell, moving my feet out of the covers. The lady has ruined my morning; and it's been the same every other morning this week. While getting ready for work, she runs around like a goddamn cat chasing its own shadow. I can hear everything.

These walls are so paper-thin I can hear the neighbors upstairs everyday without fail. Which is kind of funny. I've never met them once in all the time we've been here, yet I could tell you exactly which part of their apartment they're in at any given moment.

The wood that separates their floor from my ceiling creaks with each step.

Actually, I did see the tenant above, but only once, on a Saturday afternoon. It's a woman weighing close to 300 pounds, which explains why the floor always sounds like it's gonna collapse when she's up and about.

I think I heard her get up once while I was doing the same exact thing I'm doing right now, lying in my bed contemplating if I should move or sleep in another hour. The monster was thumping her way around my ceiling. Then I remember hearing that sound of wood straining not to crack and break in half on top of me. That quickly convinced me it was time to get up, at least that time.

A voice calls me from afar. "How many times do I have to tell ya? Get the hell up."

I must've fallen back asleep. "I heard ya the first time," I yell back.

I stand up to stretch, and head towards the bathroom. I open my door slowly, peering through the crack so I don't run into the morning demon complaining about what kind of a kid I am turning out to be.

Coast is clear through the dark hallway.

I run in, shut the door, and turn knobs in the tub for the shower.

As I wait for the hot water to kick in I think about today—senior skip day—and the fun my girlfriend and I have planned. Although I am only a high-school junior, my girlfriend is a senior and I don't like to be excluded from anything; plus, it's a nice excuse to skip another day of school.

I take a quick hot shower and run into my closet to figure out what to wear for this special occasion. My mother can't really afford to buy me clothes, but I still manage to carry some fine threads in my closet from five-finger discounts that stores around here carry daily.

And, no, I haven't been caught *yet*—that's the word everyone I know thickly underlines. They think just because their cherries have been popped in the back seat of a cop car, that my time will come. I consider that to be bullshit because most of my friends are morons. Don't get me wrong, they're cool kids and everything, just not too bright. Swiss cheese heads I like to call 'em.

The difference between them and me is that they plan what to do as they're getting caught, and this usually means to run. I plan ahead of time or look at my options for a good takedown. Actually, I've come up with my own little system, which as far as I'm concerned is flawless.

First things first. I look around for a while in the store for security guards, undercover plainclothes employees whose sole mission is to bust punks like me. To distinguish the average Joe from undercover security all you need to do is to watch people shop. When the average Mary or Joe shop, they go from aisle to aisle grabbing what they need, flitting their eyes from hand list to preservative, back to list to the back of a box of crackers. Security shops much differently. First off, they'll never have a cart, so if you got something crouched in your jeans and you see a man carrying one of those hand held carts following you around, that means you're fucked. Also, security never pays attention to what they grab from the shelves. They'll palm random items, which they toss into their hand-held basket, while their eyes crop to the side watching you plummet to destruction. Another thing to watch out for are those shelved products with man-made holes for eyeballs, which can peer to the other side of the aisle.

When all these points are checked and I am able to find the exact location of security and how far they are from the aisle of the product I need, like clothes for example, I'll throw a shirt or a coat over my own clothes. But, if it's a hat, I fold the back end into the front of the hat and place it in my armpit. It fits perfectly. Then I just walk out, maybe buy a candy bar or something small, but only if I'm under suspicion, then just walk home.

That's why each article of clothes I own has a pretty cool story that goes along with it.

I pick out a light brown button-up shirt that I stole from a friend's dad's closet. When everyone was getting fucked up and not paying attention to me, I was sane enough to wander around the house, going through closets and cabinet drawers to find something to go home with. The cool thing about this shirt struck me when I wore it for the first time; the pen pocket had two twenty-dollar bills stuck to the fabric, like the money had been washed a bunch of times, which meant that pops had forgotten about the funds, making it mine.

I throw on a pair of jeans, lace up my sneakers, and am ready to jet. But before taking off, I go to my secret stash of funds—a cigar box located secretly in my bookshelf. The cigar box is old. I found it along the side of a cigarette store, and it fits in perfectly with all the other books I've stolen from stores and people's houses. I stash my money here because if moms finds out I've got this much cash on me, she might think I have a job and can pay for my own lunch. But if she doesn't find it, and that's the plan, four dollars will be heading my way Monday through Friday.

Inside the box is a large stack of bills, amounting to about eighty dollars. I bite my lip and figure the amount I will need today, take out twenty, and put the rest back in its place. I grab my Walkman, my backpack, and one last gander in the mirror just to make sure I look okay. Then, I sit on my bed and look out my window, visualizing the day in my head.

I've never been to Anna's house before, but I picture it to be surrounded by a picket fence with green grass that extends to the floors next to the porch. I can see myself walking up and entering through the front door, enveloped by a creepy silence punctuated only by the creaks of my feet stepping on the carpet. With a smile on my face, I would take off my backpack and stand next to the rail. I climb two steps at a time, not knowing where her room would be at, but I figure it would be closest to where the sun shines the brightest. I stand next to the door, eyed by family members in frames that hang on the wall, and touch the knob. Her family would smile and accept me as I am, as if to egg me on as I start to open the bedroom door.

Just when I push, the door opens—BEEP-BEEP-BEEP.

I must've hit snooze and not the "off" button.

My dream vanishes, but the day is alive, so I figure I'd best finish my daydream in person rather than in my head; that's when I cease either to hear or to see my mom's mouth yell about how I'm late for the bus. Happiness does that to you, makes you deaf during important subconscious melodies that you create in your head. Which seems like a good thing, 'cause sadness is constantly at my doorstep. Mostly I just walk past it, having better things to do. Like walk to Anna's.

I step out into the breezy morning air. My eyes meet the sun to find my starting point for a new journey. I've walked down this path many times before, its concrete stained with chalk marks left by school children, who have drawn pictures, as we used to do, of houses we saw daily from across the creek, hoping one day we could live in places like them. But that was before the kids who lived in those houses called us names for living in the poor parts. So we were left only with the option of escaping our reality through our first mind-altering drugs and running around in circles to end the pain for a short while—until we began pushing the envelope with higher mind-altering drugs that lasted a little longer than spinning in circles.

I figure I got about a two-mile walk ahead of me. Most kids my age have cars to get around, but I ain't got the cash to buy one myself and those things are too big for me to steal. Anyways, I don't even have a license. Mom says that means responsibility, which she doesn't think I have, and maybe I agree, but it would be damn nice to drive rather than walk.

I've asked her several times if she would take me to get it, but she always says the same thing. "Whaddya think, I'm nuts? Yeah right, like I'm going to let you get behind the wheel of a car. I know what you and your so-called friends do, and anyways whose car ya' gonna drive? Don't think mine. I'm not having my car be an accessory to what ever it is you do."

She could've just said no and left it at that. But, she's all about arguing and speaking forever to make a point.

I decide the first thing I need to do before making it out to Anna's house is stop at the bus stop, buy me some weed, and relax before the long walk.

The apartment complex I live in is old; it's been up and running since the early seventies. At one point long ago, you could tell the tenants were nice. But they built this joint for families with low incomes, meaning parents who lived in the ghettos for a long time and then moved out this way to the suburbs; to give their children 'better lives, better education'. The fucked-up part is that most parents never change their ways, and most kids I know who live around these parts never take advantage of the education that's out here. They become bums, schleps; kids who just get high all day, skip school, drop out, and get into trouble. My mom says I'm falling down the same path, but I don't buy it. What I'm doing now is having fun, like all the other kids my age are doing. I am a teenager. That's the closest thing I know to invincibility—the feeling of being invincible, that is.

The complex is broken into three different parts. The one I live in is mostly filled with retired old people, so it's always quiet. When noise starts to pick up and something goes down, these people here aren't afraid to call the cops. For instance, the other day, a couple outside were having a simple argument in the parking lot. No slugging, just loudmouthed remarks from a dirty, hairy biker and his brown-toothed, bleach-blonde babe. As the sirens approached, the couple went inside their car to finish the conversation. When the cops rolled up everyone from the complex came out of their apartments like bears from hibernation to watch what they can get to see only on late night TV. Believe me when I say twenty *old* people. They stood with their walkers and respirators on the sidewalks, balconies, and doorways watching the police tell the couple to finish the argument inside. That was it. The couple went into their apartment, the cops left; but the old people had hoped for more, so they swarmed together like bees to gossip on the incident.

It's absurd how the only excitement these people get is through watching soaps and calling the cops. It's a freak show at the circus. The only cool thing about this area is that it's nicer-looking than the other complexes across the basketball court.

Walking past the pole reminds me of how this used to be a basketball court but now, with no hoop, it's just this big slab of elevated concrete that separates my complex from the others. The hoop was taken down on account of me and my friends hooking a kid up to it from his belt for like four hours. Some experience that turned out to be.

Everyone has had this done to them in the neighborhood when they were younger, especially Kenny, this weird kid from around the way. We all knew he wasn't retarded, just slow. I mean he took all the special classes at school and he did have to ride the "other" bus home, but he was fun to fuck with. Kenny was always talking about stupid shit that nobody believed—how he was a black belt in karate, or how he had all these guns stashed in his room and if anyone fucked with him they were dead. The best one was his dad being an undercover FBI agent. But the only undercover work we ever saw his father do was sit his fat ass down and drink, or sit on the sofa collecting checks for a medical problem that happened like ten years ago.

One day after school, the guys and I wanted to put Kenny's martial arts to the test. We had nothing better to do. When we saw him walking from the bus stop we yelled at him from the basketball court. "Come here for a sec."

As soon as he got close enough we all tackled him to the ground, laughing hysterically. When we got a hold of his hands, we took Rob's belt and used it to tie up Kenny's hands. Now this wasn't an easy thing to do. I mean, Kenny's like almost six foot, thin and lanky. He'd squirm around and keep getting loose, so to keep his hands together we had to tickle him on the sides. That loosened up his grip pretty quick, kind of relaxed his muscles. As soon as we got his hands tied together, we hoisted the long fucker up onto the hoop from his belt, laughing even harder as he continued to kick and scream, looking like a daddy long legs doing the roger rabbit.

"So, Kenny, why don't you use your karate now, tough guy?" Hector yelled from the ground where he lay.

"Yeah, Kenny. I thought you were some hard-ass or somethin'," yelled another kid.

"I know, guys!" Jones suddenly glinted. "Let's get a stick an' play pinata with the lanky fucker!"

Everyone was up for that, so we all got up from the ground laughing at the wiggling ant, spider down to the creek to find a long thin stick, raced back to the hoop, blindfolded each other, like a real pinata party. Then we spun each other around until we were dizzy. We gave Kenny a nice fun-whack on his legs with the stick. We were so dizzy we started whacking each other; and even when we weren't dizzy any more, we'd just whack someone for the hell of it. Shit like this even got Kenny laughing, looking like a hung fish out of water. And as we were all having fun laughing, smacking, and horsing around, the unexpected happened—Junior came strolling around and walked up to the court.

We tried to continue our fun, ignoring him. I think that just pissed him off more. He walked right between Kenny and us and said with his stupid voice. "Hey, dipshits, whaddya think ya'll doin', huh?" None of us answered. We just stared at him, waiting for him to make a move so we could run. If he wasn't so big, we might have been able to take him, but we said fuck it and kept our distance.

"Hey, asshole, give me that stick!" He went on, and wrenched it out of Hector's hands. "So this is what ya'll was doin' right-havin' fun with this retard?"

He should speak.

Junior began whacking Kenny with our stick, not so hard at first, but after each blow he'd stare at us all to prove who the bad ass was. After a couple whacks, he quit staring and started the hard hitting. You could see Kenny was holding in the tears, not only because he was getting hit badly, but because he was scared of what Junior might do next.

Well, the whacking got harder. I could see Kenny's eyes beginning to swell.

WHACK.

Junior hit him in the legs...WHACK...in the body...WHACK...and all Kenny could do was squirm and hope to get loose, but we had...WHACK...tied him up there pretty...WHACK...good...

At this point, Kenny had no choice but to start screaming his head off. The pain was unbearable. It's like when your parents smack you real hard across the rear and you get that tingly ticklish sensation you can get rid of only by rubbing your rear. Well, Kenny couldn't rub, and it was like watching someone getting tortured.

WHACK.

Between wails, he pleaded for Junior to stop, but hearing his plea for mercy only excited Junior. He began grinning that stupid-looking smile that made his teeth come out like the front end of a car. We tried helping, yelling at Junior to stop. One kid even attempted to grab the stick from him, but got smacked across the chest with it. He had to rub away his. All this time, I thought poor ol' Kenny can't even do that.

Without warning, Junior began swinging that stick at all of us, and chasing us down the street like alley cats. When we were far enough, all we could do was watch and pray this first human pinata wouldn't pop.

From where we stood, we finally saw the stick break, followed by the echoes of Kenny's cries. Junior dropped the stick's end left in his hands and ran. We rushed over to Kenny and stood uncomprehendingly right below him. We couldn't believe our eyes. Blood actually dripped from Kenny's jeans onto the concrete. Seeing concrete soaked in deep red, we ran-leaving poor old Kenny hanging by his belt screaming to the four winds.

When night fell, I remember getting a phone call from Hector telling me what had happened after we left.

"Did the fucker rat us out, Hec?"

"Naw, he jus' told his parents he was playin' around with us that's all. But, guess what the fuck happened to Ken, man," Hector said.

"What, man, what?"

"Junior, that fuckin' asshole hit Kenny so hard that one of the fucker's nuts exploded in his pants. Like a goddamn time bomb or something."

I started laughing a little but covered the phone so Hec couldn't hear.

"Yeah, man. When Ken's parents found him up on the hoop his pops took him down while his moms ran to call the ambulance. They say they found his nut, wrapped it in a napkin and took it with 'em to the hospital to see if they could reattach it, but they couldn't."

"No shit," I said in amazement.

"Yeah, but the best part, Sol, is when Kenny's dad got back to the complex, he found Junior and beat the living shit out of him, givin' Junior his own trip to the hospital." Without Hector even saying anything, I understood this to mean that Kenny's dad had gone to jail after the cops were called—as Hec, I presume, got the story when everyone had finished gossiping.

After all that bad shit happened, we all got together again to play some ball, but we noticed the hoop was gone. The circular brownish bloodstains where the hoop used to be are still there, even today.

CHAPTER 2

❈

It's always been just my mother and me.

My dad, I've never met him. My mother talks about him every now and again usually when the times in her life are really tough, and she starts mumbling about how he ruined her life, having to raise me all by herself.

I remember one Sunday when I was about ten or so, I asked mother how she met my dad (this was during a time when her and I could stand each other; this was during a time when I wasn't getting into so much trouble). Anyways, we were at this deli across the street from the apartment complex we would go to every Sunday to eat breakfast. I recall the expression on her face being somewhat surprised after I asked her the question.

"Well," she began, "I was about seventeen years old and living with my folks in Detroit; that was during a time when girls could walk down the street during the day or night and not get robbed or killed. Nowadays, you go down there in your car and you're still not safe. Anyways, a girlfriend of mine from high school knew your father, and she took him along to a school dance to meet me because she said we would be a good match. He was already outta school. I think he was working at one of those car factory plants or somethin' like that, but you could tell he made pretty good money at his job.

He drove a Camaro, had his own apartment, and dressed really good. Now, at that time, a young girl was impressed by a young man like that, who looked like he had his act together; 'cause during that time, where I grew up not too many men took care of their responsibilities. Men during that time were having babies and not taking care of them, or still living at home with their parents cause they wouldn't get a job," she said looking up at the ceiling, reminiscing.

"Your father and I fell in love right when we met...actually, it was during the first time we ever slow danced together; the stars sparkled in our eyes. At the start, he would take me to school and pick me up. All my friends thought I was so cool. He would take me out to dinner all the time, to the movies, he would wine and dine me non-stop. My parents didn't like him though; they use to tell me that he was bad news 'cause he worked in the factory. Now, my father, your grandfather, worked in a factory his whole life and he knew what kind of people worked there, especially hip young guys like your dad. All he would say is, "That guy is bad news". Your grandfather had a name for them, he called them bad asses. But, I didn't listen, I continued to go out with him anyways. About the time we stayed steady for a month, he asked me to marry him. Now I think I was eighteen then, or was I still seventeen?" She utters biting her lip. "Oh, I can't recall. Anyways, I told him I would if we could have a house out in the country since I've never been outta the city before. And before you knew it we were wed at the courthouse—not the type of wedding I was hoping for, but everyone doesn't get what they want. We bought a brand new ranch style house in this little farm town, where we had an acre lot of green grass, trees all around the home, and a dog I named Feebee who was a chocolate lab.

"After about a year or so of being married, I noticed something strange occurring with him 'cause he stopped taking me out as much and spent more time at work, tellin' me he was doin' double shifts. One day, I followed him, sat in the parking lot until he got off of work and made sure he went back to do his double shift, and guess what?" She asks as I shrug my little shoulders up high. "He wasn't working a double shift; he was going over some girl's house that he worked with at the factory. That night when he came home, I remember, right when he walked through the kitchen door, I started throwing plates at him and silverware, anything I could get my hands on that would hurt him really, really bad. He would yell, 'Damn it, have you lost your marbles? What are you doing?' And I started getting into it with him about how I saw him leave work and go to another girl's apartment. 'And don't try to lie or try to cover anything up 'cause I caught you,' I yelled, and then I called him 'a piece of crap', 'a bad husband', all the names in the book.

"Then, I ran to the phone to call my mom to come get me. That's when your father yanked the phone from my hands and told me not to go. He was crying, pleading, begging me not to leave, and of course I fell for it 'cause I was young and stupid. Later I learned it was just some guilt trip he would give me so I would feel sorry for him. He would pull something like this every time we had an argument to make me feel like the bad guy. After that we decided to have you, 'cause he said he only loved me and didn't want anyone else ever again.

"For awhile, when you were born, we started to do a lot of things together like a family should do: going to the park; having a picnic; spending more time at our family's house. But, again, when things got too normal for him he started staying out late again, and not coming home until morning. I liked to call it steady and settled. So, again, I waited in the parking lot of the factory for him to get out, but this time I had you with me in your car seat. And again, I followed him to another apartment, where a female co-worker lived and saw that he didn't leave until the morning. So, after that I got fed up and went back home, packed both of our bags, took anything worth value and put it in the trunk and drove off in my Oldsmobile; outta that town to start a whole new life for you and I", she said with a stern expression on her face.

"But, there was one thing I didn't think about when I left, and that was I never went to college, I never held a real job, and I only had enough money to last for a few days. So, I struggled for awhile; we lived with friends on and off. I couldn't go back home 'cause my parents thought I was a sinner 'cause I left my husband, and back then that was a definite no, no. So, from staying from room to room for a couple years, I worked odd jobs all over the place, and took a couple night courses just so I could learn how to do somethin'. And eventually, when I got a pretty good job, I was able to rent the place we have now, and although it's not the greatest place, it's a start," she proclaimed feeling proud.

After that, I think her and I got a little closer; we started watching TV together, sleeping in the same bed. She read me bedtime stories. She even took me to the video arcade a few times. But as I got older, I started roaming a little further past our parking lot in the apartment complex. I started running into kids I saw at school everyday. And they seemed to be a lot more fun than going home every night to watch the Cosby Show. I was getting tired of being steady and settled.

These kids who lived around the neighborhood would cross major roads by themselves, go into party stores and grocery stores and come out with hands full of candy they didn't pay for. They played practical jokes, hurt people, and thought it was funny. They were guys I looked at and wanted to be like, since there were no other male role models in my life.

And by the time high school came around, a friend of mine named Josie asked me to smoke dope with him down by the creek. At that time, I guess you could say I was a small time hoodlum, but I never messed with drugs.

I remember we were sitting on the grass. Josie pulled out cellophane that was once on a cigarette pack, filled with green buds that looked like mashed up oregano. He took out this pipe he made outta some Happy Meal toy—it was a miniature Frankenstein action figure. The top of its head was hollowed out and covered with tin foil, and in its mouth there was a drinking straw to suck on. He filled Frankenstein's head with dope. Then, putting the straw in his mouth, lit a flame over its head, and started sucking really hard until his face became shrunken in. His chest expanded out, and his eyes became watery with tears. Eventually, he let out the smoke, coughing a couple times saying, "It's good shit man, hit this." And as I put the straw to my mouth, he lit the flame for me and told me to suck when the green plant started to turn red. I could feel the smoke pass through my mouth, down my throat and into my lungs, and as I tried like hell to hold it in, I couldn't and let out a terrible cough, watching all this smoke come outta my mouth and nose.

After a few more cracks at it, I got the picture and started holding the flame myself on top of Frankenstein's head, packing the bowl when Josie told me it was "Cashed out dude!" Finally, when the high kicked in, I almost thought for a second I was dreaming, feeling a little light headed, but at the same time very very heavy—as if I gained a few pounds. I didn't think about anything when I was wasted. I didn't think about my mom and how she worked her ass off everyday so we could keep this apartment. I didn't think about how I had to work extra hard than the average kid in school, so maybe I could get a scholarship to go to college. I didn't think about where I lived. I didn't think about who I was. The only thing on my mind was thinking of myself as the breeze, like the wind just passing through everything. Not really placed in one particular area, but more like free to go and do as I please all across the world, until it was time to calm down, cash out so to speak, just to fill it and light it, and ride it all over again. And I continued to feel this way until I had my first bad trip; I started thinking about how now I was the guy leaving my mother alone at home, not returning until the next day. Telling her lies of where I was at, and eventually crying, giving her guilt trips, about how I felt so pressured—and I got away with it.

I became the same exact man my mother hated, the man I had never met in person; and how my friends acted you could almost tell that my father was their father too. At that point, I stopped caring. I looked ahead and saw no real future, just the consequences I faced of being born. Now, I feel all that will change with the help of Anna, who motivates me to be a better person.

CHAPTER 3

❀

Passing the bus stop through the basketball court, in and out of the apartment buildings until I walk out the other end into the jungle gym, I see someone sitting on the other side on a balcony. Nobody relaxed outside this early in the morning—unless you were Hec. His backpack lies next to him and smoke rises around his head. His position and the exact moment in time tell me he's skipping, too.

I walk up to the rail and drop my book bag on the grass along the way.

"What's up?" I ask, leaning against the balcony.

He starts shuffling through his pockets and pulls out a pack of cigarettes, throws me one and says, "Need a light?"

"Yeah," I answer, and just as quickly a flame ignites under my chin. "Why aren't you at the bus stop today? Goin' to school?"

"Hell, no!" He answers. "Man, it's senior-skip day. If those bums don't hafta go, neither do I."

I shake my head in agreement. "I ain't goin' today either. Anna and I decided to hang out."

"Oh, is that the new one?" He asks.

I shake my head again in agreement, taking a drag from the cigarette.

"Oh yeah, I almost forgot to tell ya', Jug just got a shit load of weed. I think I'm gonna hang out there."

I continue smoking.

"Hey, screw your woman, man. Come hang with us, get high all day."

"Naw," I blow smoke out my nose. "We've been planning this for a coupla' weeks now. Anyways, smokin' weed with Jug and his pops all day gets old after a while."

A smile reflects off of Hector's face. He knows I'm right. "Whatever, man. It's not like I got other shit planned for today. Besides, nothing feels better than being high all day long. Numb the pain, amigo," he says, trying to look world-weary.

Hector—I've known him forever. He's probably the only kid that I trust and consider a real friend. He's lazy, rarely goes to school. And his mom hates his guts. She always throws his ass out of the apartment after a fight, and he wanders in the street for a little while, but he always ends up knocking on my bedroom window to crash for the night. I never turn him down. Hell, the fucker's got his own little spot in my room, with blankets and pillows from home stuffed in the corner next to my bed. He's not a bad-looking kid, either, but for some reason he's real gawkish with the ladies-shy and passive as hell. I always hoped he'd find some girl that would change him around, like Anna does for me, or at whose house he might even end up sleeping every night, instead of mine. But, I know that will never happen, I know I'm all he's got.

"Hey, Hec, I was thinking about buying some shit before I begin walkin'. It's like two miles away and I'll smoke some wit cha before I take off."

"Cool. Let's go wake up Jug."

He hops over the rail and we start walking to Jug's, leaving our bags outside—nobody's gonna steal them 'cause nobody around here goes to school.

Jug—what a piece of shit! His head has these nasty brown curls that shine from not showering. He says all the oil that builds up in your hair allows the weed to linger longer in your brain. That's Jug. It's all bullshit; he's just too fuckin' lazy to take a shower. But what's more disgusting is that all the grease from his head shining along his forehead makes his head even fatter than it already is. The only cool thing about him—besides all the weed he smokes with us—is that he's one of the last burnouts that crossed over to become a wigger, you know one of those guys that tries to act and be black. He's got this really bad mullet cut, which he tries to hide with a baseball cap covered with rhinestones. And he claims the best thing that ever happened in history was the collaboration between Public Enemy and Anthrax with "Bring the Noise"—his pretense of a silly cross-cultural style.

Hector informs me on the walk over that we will have to knock on the basement window instead of the front door. I guess his pop likes to sleep late, since neither of them have a job; if we wake him up, he'll come at us with a hammer. That fat fucker hates our guts, though I don't really blame him. I mean I'd be pissed off all the time, too, if I was that ugly. The funny part is that Jug looks exactly like his dad, except fatter and more paranoid—especially when we come by to pick up some shit. His dad is always telling him that we're all morons and that they'll get busted one day for messing with us. But Jug doesn't listen.

A couple of weeks ago, Jug's dad went out for the night and Jug decided to throw a party, a small little get together. But everyone got trashed, and we started to get a little rowdy, waking up the neighbors, you know, shit like that. The cops showed up, and everyone ran out the balcony window and left Jug all by himself to deal with them. Ten minutes later, Jug's pops showed up while the police were checking out the situation, and they watch him go into the apartment. Realizing of course that this was the same house they got the call for, they went to the door. Just as they were ringing the doorbell, Jug was flying through the screen door running for his life from his pops, who was wielding a hammer, having just seen the mess.

Well, the cops quickly discovered Jug's dad was way over the legal drinking limit and hauled his fat ass to jail, and it was up to Jug to bail his pops out. But before he did, the kid smoked like a pound of weed, knowing full well that when he got his dad out, he was getting a good beating.

A couple of days later we saw Jug with a black eye and swollen cheeks. He told us we weren't allowed over anymore. But, when his pops realized we were the only kids who pretty much bought from him, we were all allowed back into his house to get high that same week.

Hec and I walk up to the basement window, give it a couple good whacks and wait. A few moments later we see these eyes glow from the other side of the window like those of a cat. The window pops open and I drop twenty bills down into it. Jug closes the window without a hint of acknowledgment and we wait a couple more minutes.

"So, Sol, you think ya' gonna' get laid tonight?"

"I don't know. I don't really care Hec. I kinda' dig this girl; she's not like all the others we know. She kinda' shows me things we'd never see around this shit hole. It's like she's showing me how to escape—be like…responsible…"

We pause.

You can tell Hector begins thinking about this-that "something out there" that he's never seen. We both shut up and ponder a better life than this one. To be honest, if it came right up to our faces in Technicolor—so we could touch it, feel it, smell it—we probably still wouldn't take it. We would be too scared, I guess. It'd be like a dream that felt so real we wouldn't wanna' wake up from it. But, we do. Just like this morning and every other morning. This is where we always end up.

So, there we stand, outside a basement window, waiting for our drugs, knowing how it takes the pain away, and sends us back to our dreams...for a little while.

"Oh, yeah," Hec interrupts our daydreaming. "Leave your window open tonight; I don't think I feel like sleeping at home."

"Okay. No problem man. You know I gotcha back to infinite."

"Thanks, kid."

The basement window swings open and out flies a small little baggie. I walk a few steps towards it, pick it up from the lawn, and bring it closer to my eyes, because I don't recognize the shit that's inside.

I walk back to the basement window and start knocking on it, yelling, "Jug, ya' crackhead fuck! You gave me the wrong shit. I want some weed, not coke."

The window opens back up and I throw the shit inside, starting to get a little upset, because I don't want to be late, or sober, for the long walk. It's not that I don't do coke—I do—but only on special occasions.

Two seconds later the right bag flies out. I pick it up and put the shit in my shoe. Hec walks over to the window to tell Jug he'll be over later, and how senior-skip day will be fun today. After they're done conversing, we walk back to Hec's and decide that's where we're gonna' smoke 'cause his mom's at work.

We enter from the backdoor of his apartment complex. The dim light bulbs glare all the way down the empty hallway to the front entrance. As we walk to his door, we hear babies crying, TVs blaring, and the aroma of morning breakfast looms in the dark gloomy space. Hec pulls out his house key from a dirty old shoelace connected to his neck, jiggles the door a few times to the left, and a soft sounded ping comes from the lock.

We walk in.

His apartment has the exact same layout as ours. Light vanilla-painted walls, the closet immediately to the right when you enter the front door (which is off its track and hanging sideways), and the ledge built right in front of the door no taller than my chest and filled with white candles in glass holders.

I pop off my shoes and head towards the living room, which is completely covered with plants along the walls. I plop myself down on the couch and realize this living room is the perfect atmosphere for smoking weed; it feels safari, and his mom's got the heat cranked up so high I'm about to break out in a sweat. Hector is in the kitchen looking for something to eat, as I pull out the bag from my shoe and begin the ritual of rolling a joint.

"Man, this woman never shops. Damn!" Hec yells angrily as he slams the pantry shut, walks into the living room carrying a half-empty bag of bread, and takes a seat on the Lazy Boy chair next to the couch. He then grabs a slice of bread, rips the green off the corners, and sticks the rest in his mouth. It was disgusting to look at, but I go back to rolling up the tea.

"It's okay, man. I only like the middle part anyways," he says.

"I don't think I can allow ya' to hit my joint with all that green bread bacteria hanging from your lip. I ain't catchin' that shit," I insist.

He gives me a suspicious look, says, "Fuck you," and smirks at me, knowing I'm just messing around.

I light a flame under the Thai stick and start puffing until the flame travels from the lighter to the joint. I inhale the first hit and keep it there for a long time, until I start to feel in my lungs that it wants to come out. But I desperately hold it in, clamming my mouth shut. After stifling myself for so long, I burst out in a cough like crazy. Saliva quickly forms in my mouth. My eyes dilate, turning into water.

I know the feeling is coming, so I pass it over to Hec.

"Hey, Solomon, I've come to a crossroads in my life. I've decided I want to be a millionaire," he says. He lays low across the chair staring at the wall in the dining room. I notice a smirk plays across his face. "Yeah, man, it's my time to shine—a dream told me so last night."

I look over at him, roll my eyes, and continue to stare at the wall with my own smirk. I know he was waiting for me to ask what the dream was about, but honestly at this point I couldn't care less. I look over at him from the corners of my eyes and see that he's getting antsy for me to ask.

I keep him suspended. A few more moments later, he says, "yeah kid, it was a pretty interesting dream. Oh, yeah."

Silence.

"Yup, it told me a lot, man."

I begin to get annoyed. I really don't want to hear about it, but seeing no exit, I ask with a slow drawn-out gesture, "Oookay, maaaan, what's the dream about?"

Hec sits up in his chair looking at me for clear understanding, thinking I'm gonna' pay attention.

"Ok, this dream, right, wasn't one of those normal ones. I mean, seriously. It was like I was…you know, touching everything…feeling it like I was awake." His hands grope the chair for visuals. "Okay, I was walkin' home and it was late. I mean really late…and foggy too. I'm talkin' so foggy you couldn't see your hand in front of your fuckin' face."

He brings his hand up to his grinning face, trying to reenact the experience. He had no idea how bad I wanted to just smack his hand into his face.

"Well I was walkin' home through the jungle gym," he goes on. "I trip over somethin', and I fuckin' drop like a brick onto the grass. So, while on the ground, I start searching for whatever I tripped on, and I finally find it: this big-ass rock. For some reason, though, somethin' in my head tells me to get a closer look at it, so I pull out my lighter and hold the torch to the stupid thing. It was this pure white, smooth rock with little notches in the middle. When I pull the lighter closer to these marks, I swear ta God, I saw numbers carved into the fucker. Then a second later, the metal top of my lighter got so fuckin' hot that I dropped the lighter on the ground, and I woke up."

I look at him funny. "What the fuck does that have ta do with anything about dollars?"

"Whaddya mean, moron? Weren't ya' listenin?" He replies.

"Guess not!"

"Those notches in the rock, stupid, they were numbers, ya know. Lottery numbers. I'm gonna send Jug to buy me a ticket later…and win my millions."

I look over at him and burst out laughing. He sits there with a confused look on his face. Calming down, I return to my slouching position on the couch and grin. "Okay, Hec, whatever man. That sign's really fuckin' cool," rolling my eyes again and shake my head.

Ruffled, Hec says, "Well, asshole, if you're such a smart guy, what the fuck are *you* gonna' do with your life?"

I look at him with a straight face and answer, "What? Be a millionaire!"

We both burst out in laughter, realizing how full of shit we both are. When our laughter died down, we sank back lazily to enjoy the rest of our comatose state before it dies away.

And it does, as it has to. The life inside us dead, we come down from the high. Two beings moved and motivated by nothing.

Outside, the sun has hidden behind one of the buildings, filling the room with dark sharp shadows. There's a gray, sad feeling inside me, as I move my eyes seemingly for the first time in years. Hector is completely knocked out on the chair, his eyelids trembling. I think he's dreaming—my sign to get up.

I quietly peel myself off the couch and rise; it is like reaching for the sky. Feeling lightheaded, I think of how this day is starting. Instead of an alarm clock, my ambition, my purpose for today is waking me up, and her name is Anna and she makes me happy.

I put my shoes on, pull out a sheet of paper from my book bag and write Hec a note. *Hec, if you need me I'll be at Anna's*; and I write down the number. I tiptoe closer to him and place the paper on his chest, tiptoe back to the door and quietly walk out.

CHAPTER 4

❀

Walking through the neighborhood behind the apartments, I decide to pass through some back streets instead of the main road; during the day, the police monitor the streets, looking for kids like me to bust. If you get picked up by the police when you're supposed to be in school, they'll give you a ticket for loitering and *drive* you to school, who will in turn call your parents, and give you detention for like a month. It's like getting fucked twice in one day.

    A typical day of school for me isn't very productive in the conventional sense of the term. I mean, in my mind, I feel I get a lot accomplished, but it's not really school work. Usually, when I get to school, around seven in the morning since first period begins at 7:15 AM, I hang out in the English hallway, where I sit against the lockers with Hector and Josie, and scheme up a plan to get me outta' school for lunch. This extra planning is necessary, due to the security guards that linger around the hallways all day. They were hired a couple years back after the population of our high school doubled, making it a little harder to keep an eye on all the kids.

    My first period for the day is American History with Ms. Stellar and Mrs. Gains. It's two classes put together. There's like sixty kids total in the classroom. What's nice about this is if I decide to skip, I usually go unnoticed 'cause I just ask someone to yell "here" when they call my name from role call, and I sit so far back in the classroom that they wouldn't be able to tell if that was me saying here or not. For about one hour, I joke around with this other high-on named Chad. He's this really dopey type kid who'll do just about anything if you ask him to. He's got this short bleach-blonde hair, a big Jewish nose, and zits all across his face—big ones like the size of pepperonis probably from not washing. He's the kid in class that makes practical jokes to piss off the teacher. He's the kid in class that will raise his hand every second if he doesn't understand every part of the lesson, when the problem is he just doesn't get *anything*. Then, he gets thrown out of class for the rest of the hour 'cause he can't calm down. Usually, him and I just talk about the rituals and practices we do to get high. We debate about how to roll a joint, explain the processes of making a bowl for dope when you don't have one handy, and glamorize stories which, I think, half of the shit *he* says is made up. When the bell rings, I run outta' class, and outside to this tree that everyone goes to have a smoke. Daily, in between classes, you can see at least a hundred kids hanging out here to light up before the next class. The people who are on the outside perimeter of this huge group are the ones who watch for security and yell when they see them coming outta the building, which means dropping your cigarette to the ground and walking back to school. But, if you're an experienced smoker like myself you won't have to drop your smoke. What I do is cup it in the inside of my palm, and stick my hand in my pocket without burning myself. The only down spot to doing this is your hand stinks like smoke forever and the smell won't wash off very easily with just soap and water. But, I guess that's the price you pay to serve your nicotine fit.

 Second period is English Literature with Mr. Harris. This class is actually pretty cool because for a whole hour all we do is read short stories or books, then watch the movie that was made from one of the books we just read. I don't mind reading.

The class consists of mostly high school seniors, who need to take a blow off class just to graduate. Maybe that's why I like this class so much because it's a jerk-off class that allows me to just drift around through other people's lives for an hour and not have to think about where I'm at right now. Tom Sawyer—now that was a good book.

When the high school year books came out, I remember this girl asked me to sign hers. I'm not really much for words, so what I did was stick my hand on one of the pages, and draw the outline of my hand. Then, I just drew some weird trippy picture inside. Everyone in my English class thought it was really cool, and the rest of the kids asked me to do the same thing in their yearbook. When the bell rings for the end of that class, I run back out to the tree, catch a smoke, talk with a few kids, and walk back behind the school, make sure the coast is clear, and sprint across the football field to meet up with Charlie behind the bleachers. Both of us have study hall for 3rd period, which pretty much is a class to do homework in, if and only if you get kicked out of your real class for too many absences. Since all we do is sit around anyway, Charlie thought it would be good exercise to walk to 7–11 everyday, smoke a joint, a couple cigarettes, and buy a Slurpee. By the time we walk there and back, it's about time for fourth period, which I go to everyday now cause Anna's in that class.

A couple months back, Charlie and I were walking through the woods to go to 7–11. We were smoking a fat joint, finishing this monster sucker off. I mean, like putting the thing out when out from nowhere walks a security guard. Usually, in situations like this I would just run for dear life back to school and hide in one of the boys' bathrooms until I feel the coast is clear, but this time Charlie and I were so blitzed that we just stood there, staring at him as he walked up to us, and asked us what we were doing. Of course, since both of us were retarded, we gave him answers like "I dunno" and "Whaddya mean?" Shit like that until he started sniffing the air like a hound dog, asking us who was smoking. Of course, we shrugged like we didn't know what he was talking about, but for the rest of the walk back to school, he kept asking us if we were sure we weren't smoking. Then, instead of suspending us, which I hoped for, they decided to give us in-school suspension, which means sitting in a classroom all day long, without moving from our seats until the last bell of the day rings. So, if you go to my school, and you want a day off to spend at home, you do something bad, but there might be a chance you'll get in-school suspension all day instead of out of school suspension. It's a risk.

For fourth period, I meet up with Anna in the library, where we just hold hands for a few minutes, kiss a little, and walk to class. This is the only class that I pull out my notebook, pay attention, and listen to the lecture for the whole hour. I do this only because I'm with Anna and that's what she does, but if she wasn't with me, I probably wouldn't show up.

For lunch, I try to find someone with a car to drive me out and take me to McDonald's or something like that. I usually want to go with someone I can get messed up with, but if no one is available I'll just go for the pure pleasure of getting outta school for a while. If nothing is going on after lunch, then I'll go back to school, but if friends are hanging out or doing something like that, I'll take the rest of the day off.

Fifth Period used to be Algebra, but of course I missed so many times that I was kicked out and set with another study hall. The funny part about this class was that before I got booted out, the principal used to send notes to me everyday from another student, informing me that I was called to the office. I knew that it was to kick me out of class. So, what I did was take that little pink slip that the student gave me, tell em I'll be there in a few minutes, then, stayed in class without leaving. Or using that as a pass to leave class for a while and walk around the halls till the end of class. Although this worked five different times, by the sixth, I must of been on his shit list cause he actually came to my classroom and dragged me out, escorting me to the office, and having me sign some documents that I will fail Algebra, and no longer attend that class. Since I don't know anyone who's in study period with me, I'll either go and read a book, or go to the bathroom, sit on a stall for an hour, and read a book. It all depends on the mood.

By Sixth period, I'm anxious to get home, so I just sit in the back of my Biology class and stare at the clock, waiting for it to hit 2:30. And when that bell rings I run to the bus, and get to a phone to call Anna, or get high, or hangout with friends accomplishing not one piece of homework, or studying one book. By the time tests come, I'm so unprepared that I just guess on all the answers, and skip that next day of class, so I don't have to look in the eyes of my teachers when they show off their look of disappointment.

I zip through blocks of barking dogs and sprinkler systems and come across what looks like a corner flower shop. Compared to the huge homes right next door to it, it is a puny one-story building with large, bright-green vines covering the exterior, which doesn't fit the layout of the rest of the block. Most of the homes around the shop are large two-story homes with columns in the front entrance, covered in white paint and green grass trimmed to perfection. Then, you have this old brick building meshed with vines, colorful flowers sitting outside, and huge square windows, where more flowers sit in the sun. Despite the motley look, this combination of styles gives the block a nice cozy feeling that something old was being remembered and not torn down.

I walk closer, where housewives saunter around with nothing better to do than buy flowers, hoping maybe some day they'll have their garden photographed in Better Homes, or some shit like that.

I step inside to buy some flowers for Anna, like a surprise or something. It was right out of an old fifties black-and-white movie. The door hit a bell hanging up on top. A little old woman is at the counter and a man walks away saying, "Thanks again, Alice. I wouldn't know what I'd do if this place wasn't here."

"No problem. I'll probably see you next week," she answers in soft country-grandma drawl.

I begin looking around checking out the different flowers, making a show of reading the little cards next to them with their names. Honestly, I don't know what Anna likes. There's so much of a selection here that my ADD kicks in, making it even harder to decide. I have the same problems when it comes to restaurant menus because sometimes there are so many things to choose from that I can't decide what looks better than the next thing on the menu.

I keep circling around the shop hoping that something might catch my eye and I could grab it, because I know that old lady is watching me. She probably thinks I'm a moron who has no idea what his girlfriend likes. Eventually, the lady walks around the counter and stands next to me as I gaze at the fridge's contents.

"May I help you, young man?"

"I think so," I say shyly.

"Well, you've come to the right place, 'cause flowers is really what I know," she replies with a giggle, which soothes my nerves.

A smile breaks from my lips. "I was looking for...," I begin haltingly, "somethin' nice for my girlfriend."

"Do you know what kind of flowers she likes?"

I shake my head.

"Huh. Well, how about red roses? Those are perfect for any occasion, and believe me nobody goes wrong when you pick these."

She steps over to the end of the fridge, opens the door, and pulls out a bouquet of deep red roses. "Now, if anyone gave me something like this..." she says, staring at the beauty in her hand. "...I would know this person would be special."

Looking at the roses, the only thing that comes to mind is Anna, and perfection and beauty—exactly what I experience when I'm with her. She shows me that there's beauty in the world, and this is pretty much the first leap, my first step to having something that isn't used or damaged. Something I have that I didn't need to steal. She is showing me a life I've never seen before that goes beyond broken down cars and run down apartment buildings. When I'm with her I think of doing that one good deed that would wipe my list as clean as that of a boy scout. The problem is I haven't found what that big deed could be. I mean it would have to be pretty huge to make my slate clean. I giggle to myself, thinking of helping old ladies across the street or freeing a cat that's caught in a tree. Then I say, "I've never seen anything so beautiful before. I'll take 'em."

Before returning to her counter to wrap them up, she steps closer and hands a rose to me, then watches the expression of utter amazement on my face. I grab it from the stem, forgetting it has thorns, and feel sharpness sink into my flesh like broken glass. I let go suddenly. The rose drops to the floor and its petals fall off leaving it wounded like a small puppy. It was like a reflection; my own life crumbling to the ground.

The flesh of my hand begins to bleed.

"Come on, God," I say to myself, "why can't I have a chance, I'm tryin', man, I'm really tryin' to do right. Please, just give me a chance."

I look up at the ceiling to acknowledge Him, as if to identify whom I'm talking to out of respect. There is no reply. It is like every other time I've looked up.

The old lady walks me behind the counter to the back of the store, softly places my hand under the sink to let the cold water wash away the blood. After that, she grabs a bandage. She covers my wound, and just like a grandmother she says things like, *Oh, it'll be okay, son. And it doesn't look too bad. You'll be okay.*

I apologize for ruining one of her flowers, but she doesn't seem to mind too much. We continue looking at the red roses I want for Anna.

I end up picking a dozen beautifully opened, long-stem roses, and as the old lady goes behind the counter to wrap them up, I continue looking around.

"So, how long have you worked here?" I ask while peering at the stuffed animals in the back corner.

"Oh, I'm not sure," she replies in disbelief. "My husband and I bought this place when he retired as a little something to keep us busy, but that was quite a while ago. Do you like flowers?" she asked.

"Um, I don't know."

"Do you go to school?"

"Yeah. Around here."

"Do you like it?"

"It's okay."

"Well, shouldn't a young man like yourself be there right now?"

"Yeah, but today is senior skip day."

"Oh, I see. That must be fun. I remember when I was younger and did things like that."

When she says that I look over at her, trying to think what it would be like having fond memories. The thought quickly fades when I hear the register click and bleep for the amount I owe.

I pull out my money and look at the flowers. They are beautifully wrapped in nice light blue paper. I hand her the money, and she rings it up and hands me my change. As I grab the flowers, and turn towards the door, she asks.

"I was wondering, young man, do you have a job?"

"Naw," I answer.

"I was thinking about finding some help...would you be interested?"

"Sure. I guess." I smile in amazement.

"Well, what's your name?"

"Solomon."

"My name's Alice, and from the looks of it, I can tell you'd be a pretty good boy to work at my shop." I'm not in front of a mirror or anything. When she says that my eyes grow to the size of apples. I can't believe my ears. She actually thinks I look like a good boy. No one's ever told me something like that before.

Matter of fact, I've never had a job.

I walk back to the counter telling her lies about myself. Like how I go to school everyday, study real hard, and stay outta trouble. The funny thing is, she sees right through that, telling me how she has sons and I make the same face as they do when I lie.

"I'm offering you this job, Solomon, because young kids like yourself can always learn something new, no matter what you do. I think you need to learn something...Something that will make you happy, like flowers."

A sneaky grin escapes my lips and I look up at her. I come clean about everything except the drugs, of course. I tell her where I live, how I skip school all the time, and the dumb things I do with my friends after school. She tells me this might keep me busy and out of trouble, and of course I agree. I tell her I've never been so happy in all my life as I do now. I can't believe someone sees good in me, I say to myself. Hell, I don't even see it.

She begins explaining to me how she's been through it all and how through those tough times others found it in their hearts to help her when she needed it. Now, she wants to return the favor. She has found a place in her heart to help a kid like me, without knowing a thing about me. I guess the type of things grandmothers like to do-at least that is all I could figure out for the reason of her kindness.

"Solomon, come back here Sunday morning and we'll start your training. You'll soon learn flowers are the best remedy for any trouble or sickness."

"Thank you," I tell her with a smile and walk out of the shop. "I'll see ya Sunday, ma'am, and I won't let you down."

"I know, dear. I know you won't."

As I close the door behind me, the sun shines in my face. Happiness has just sunk into my soul, and I start walking down the street.

My own mom doesn't treat me like that. I think again of Alice, and how her sons must be the happiest people in the world to have a mother like that.

My walk took on a slight skip. I was engrossed in my thoughts. All this good stuff began with Anna, I mumble to myself. My way out of the hole I'm in is getting closer. I'm getting a chance.

I quickly apologize to the man above for calling Him names for not answering my call, and jump right back to thinking about Anna. I can't wait to get to her house, to tell her the good news.

CHAPTER 5

❦

The first time I met Anna I was sitting in the back of my history class reading a book. I couldn't say for sure, but I think it was J. D. Salinger's *A Catcher in the Rye*. This is usually how I spend my day at school: either daydreaming or checking out a library book, which would be read by the last class the same day. It's not like I hate every subject on my semester schedule. The teachers, I'd have to say, are a big factor.

Like my History class.

That guy is all about leaning his lazy ass against the podium and using his red laser pointer on the projection screen like it was a light saber. Now, I know I'm not the smartest kid on the block, but those teachers are supposed to be inspiration for us kids, you know, for when we eventually ventured out into the real world. I thought they got into teaching because they enjoyed explaining their subjects with enthusiasm.

Not Mr. Gibbons. Hearing him run his mouth and watching as he slouches against the podium is like listening to an old funeral-home director trying to explain the concept of death in the sad monotony and looks of Alfred the Butler. It gets worse when he has to kick himself mentally in the butt just to blurt out simple words like "if" or "but".

That day when class was about to begin, in walked a classmate. I remember she stopped in the middle of the aisle looking for an open seat. I usually paid little attention to anyone walking in, but our class was in the high-school theater and the huge spotlights lurking above splattered all over her like a coat of fresh paint. The bright lights that splashed, baroque-like, onto her dark skin made the smallest lint pieces glow around her like stardust. I gazed over my book and mentally broke down every element of her body. Her soft dark brown hair curled up underneath her chin, covering her dimples and threw shadows on her hands softly resting on the straps of her backpack.

Still hunting for an empty seat, she moved her head back and forth, sweeping the room with her eyes, which eventually fell upon me. Immediately, she squinted as she pinpointed her place for the next forty minutes. I threw a glance down at the empty seat next to me and quickly went back to my book. But, Holden Caulfield might as well have been speaking from a distant galaxy-blah, blah, blah. She was so pretty I had forgotten how to read.

She began walking slowly towards me like a dream amongst dreams, and again I looked up and returned to my book. Then, she dropped her book bag next to mine. I felt kind of bad for her having to set such a nice looking bag next to my piece of shit with a filthy, mute green coating that use to be red when I stole it, but puke is hard to get off.

Any ways, she sighed somewhat loudly, pulled out her pen and notebook, slid her skirt under her hands, and looked forward at the screen. Meanwhile, I went unnoticed.

Mr. Gibbons, our history teacher, started taking roll call, as I pondered a line to start a simple conversation with her.

I knew that if she felt the same way I did about this teacher, she would be more than pleased to fill the void.

Before I even opened my mouth, I had to come up with something witty to say without looking stupid, so I looked for some catchy words in my book, hoping they'd fit in and sound pleasing in my opening line.

The room seemed to be heating up. During roll call, for some odd reason, I heard every laggard *here* and *present* like a drum beat in perfect tandem.

Shawns—thumpty, thump. McDonald—thumpty, thump. Patricks—thumpty, thump.

My heart was beating faster and faster to this imaginary beat. Henry—thumpty, thump.

"What's wrong with me?" I said to myself.

"Did someone just turn up the heat?"

I was getting so warm, I felt my face become red, which in turn made it very hard to think. So many thoughts racing through my brain and I could hardly hold on to a single one. It was like my brain had a mind of its own.

The little man at the podium steadily yelled out names, as students responded, maintaining the beat that thumped in my heart. My eyes began to wander around the class. I couldn't see one eyeball that wasn't pointed to the teacher. Everyone listening. Everyone being a good student.

Finally, cooking like a Thanksgiving dinner, nervous, shy, high from a joint I had smoked barely twenty minutes before class, I said, The hell with it. I turned my head towards her and uttered the phonetic equivalent of what even the dumbest primate alive wouldn't have said. Having no idea of what I've just verbalized, I gained comfort from the fleeting thought that it must have meant something. Maybe it wasn't proper English, like most normal human beings would've said it, but fuck it! I stared at her any ways expecting a reply.

Silent so far, Anna parted her beautiful lips, showing off her pearly whites and answered, "I'm fine, how are you?" She smiled. The way she looked at me left me twisted like a rubber band.

I was hypnotized.

"I'm alright," I remember answering, returning her smile and turning studiously and sagely back to my book, grateful for proof that I had uttered something meaningful after all.

Reflecting on what to say next, I wondered if I was bothering her. I figured I could at least ask something about school, something that both of us could relate to. Yeah that's it, I'll ask her about notes and the class I missed last week.

Again, I pulled my eyes away from the book I was holding in my hands and this time leaned over, closer to her, and quietly asked, "Hey, could I borrow your kiss from last week?" When I moved back to my side of the table, the words suddenly registered in my head, and my eyes grew big.

I saw myself turning into a lemon.

I was high and my creative third eye was on a mission to generate crazy pictures in my head.

My eyes kept growing bigger from sheer embarrassment at my Freudian. Finally, I looked dumb. I waited for a nonchalant *fuck you* or *you're an asshole* barely more audible than a whisper, without disturbing the class, but it never came.

Instead, as I peered from the corners of my eyes, I saw that Anna was laughing, giggling softly, both hands covering her nose and mouth. I turned to her with a blank expression, acting like I hadn't the faintest idea what I had just done, ready to confess insanity.

Well, she beat me to it and leaning sideways, said, "You asked me for a kiss. I hope you meant notes."

As I broke out in laughter, my hands kept my mouth from pissing off all the prospective history scholars around us. But I had already turned so red that she busted out laughing, and seeing her, I couldn't contain myself. It was like a chain reaction. We both laughed uncontrollably. The other students all turned to stare at us, whispering in each other's ears, and all I could think of was just letting myself go laughing out loud. I'm gonna flunk this class any ways—fuck it. *Why don't you write this in the history books, you boring old man?*

With the volume in his class knocked up a few notches and echoing off the walls, Mr. Gibbons booted us both out, "and don't you return before settling down." We both grabbed our book bags chuckling, mostly from the embarrassment, and led ourselves in our temporary insanity through the hallways. We bounced from cafeteria to hallway to another hallway, talking and learning about each other. We ended up smoking in the ladies and men's rooms and skipping the rest of the day. When history class was over, we even set up times to hang out and I guess you could say the rest was history.

CHAPTER 6

❦

Reaching the corner of Anna's street, I come across a billboard that says *Time Lost Never Found*. I try to come up with an understanding of what strikes me as a deep philosophical message. Matching ideas keep floating in my head, but I just can't decipher it. Four little words and I don't get it!

The muscles in my stomach begin to tighten; my bones rattle from the adrenaline rush of walking up to Anna's porch. I feel like a caffeinated birthday boy wired only to find out what I'm gonna receive for gifts. I get this way when something new in my life happens—uncharted territory. I'll admit that I'm a little scared. I mean, last night before hitting the sack, Anna called me and said that I should just walk in and head upstairs to her room. She told me not to worry, because her dad would be away for the week on business. The part about the parents is what makes me shaky.

I remember a while back last winter I was dating a girl named Paula who told me pretty much the same exact thing, but the outcome wasn't pretty.

Paula was grounded for throwing a party at her house, which had ultimately involved the police. She had asked me if I wanted to come over and hang out, 'cause her pops was out with his girlfriend for the night.

"Right on," I remember saying. "I'll be over right away." I hung up the phone, ventured out in the white snow-filled trees and neighborhood street lamps, and I rang the doorbell. Paula greeted me warmly from the cold air with a big smile and hug. Then, she took me by the arm and dragged me upstairs to her room, pleased that I had brought music with me to make a mix tape.

Her room was dressed for a princess, the walls painted with light shades of pink, and against them white dressers and cabinets fused against each corner allowing the morning light to reflect off the furniture. In the middle of the room, a white veil canopy enveloped her bed. I guess it was there to make the room look nice, look elegant, but I just thought of it as a way to keep out insects. Like those tents people use in the summer time that's draped with huge wire screens to keep out the mosquitoes.

We sat on her carpet skimming through cassette jackets and listening to the other tapes. Naturally, she preferred the cheesy songs to record on our tape. It didn't matter to me. I just wanted to see her somewhere other than school. Playing our music, she started to move her lips with the singer and stared at me with that glow in her eye. Soon enough, we started necking and smacking lips.

This made the vibe heat up from the bass of the music. Hungrily, we both stripped each other of our clothes, but always moving in sync with the melody. Her carpet, I remember, was soft like velvet on my back, and whenever I moved from side to side faint whispers of pleasure escaped her red mouth onto my neck.

The bass bumped harder and harder toward the song's climax. As she lay on top of me, shirtless and soft, the carpet was alive with vibrations on my back. The entire floor continued to vibrate, until we realized it wasn't the bass from the music that was creating this earthmoving experience, but the garage door opening up right below us. *Oh, shit!* I remember yelling while pushing Paula off me, then fumbling around the room looking for my shirt. She scanned the room desperately trying to figure out a proper escape route so I wouldn't get beat up.

"Go out the window in my brothers room," she said. "You can sit on the small roof under his window until the garage door closes, then jump off."

I felt a little queasy about this move. I could get hypothermia sitting out in the cold. Or, it could have been the chance of someone spotting me on his roof, thinking I was a thief, they could call the cops or worse yet start pulling out the guns; meanwhile Paula doesn't make a peep and lets me get shot down just so she won't get grounded. I'll be dead, and who's gonna hear my side of the story. I'll go down in history as a stalker, having climbed up a window sill and peeping through their daughter's window for a glimpse of young flesh. *"I don't know what he was doing up there, Daddy…I was just listening to music,"* she might say.

As I'm thinking this, Paula opened the window and pushed me out beneath the frozen sky. I sat down slanted along the roof as her window firmly locked and its shades were pushed down. I started shaking as my jeans absorbed ice and snow.

All I need to do is jump off and run home, I said to myself. Just before I moved to execute *her* escape plan, I heard shoveling below me. But I was already sliding downwards. I grabbed the awning in time. Feeling frostbitten, I looked down and saw Paula's father shoveling snow right below me, my feet dangling only a couple feet above his head.

All he needs to do is look up and I'm dead, so I did what any man in this situation would do: pray.

"Please, God, don't let him see me, whatever it is you want me to do, I'll fucking well do it."

Hanging like a piece of clothing, eyes closed, hands numb, I heard the garage door close. I took that as my signal to let go and fall on my back into the freshly made snow mound, cold and with the wind knocked out of me. I got up quickly and began running in my stiff frozen jeans, thinking how lucky I was to get out. I was running frozen, and all I thought about was that this girl is too much trouble. I never spoke to her again after that.

    Slowly, I turn the knob of the old door of Anna's house and push forward, biting my lip and snapping my eyes at each creak the wood floor makes with every step. Any second now, I'm expecting a baseball bat to the head or a gun shot wound to my chest, knowing my bad luck with home-alone daughters and busy-type fathers. To my satisfaction, the dining room table at the other end of the hall is filled with sunshine and bright rays filter through the open curtain windows.

    I slide my body between the crack of the door, close it quietly, and walk past the hallway, making a sour face with each step as the wood floors continue to creak and creak. Heading towards the staircase, I tiptoe up the stairs passing one family picture after another. Finally, I walk into her room and fix my eyes on the sleeping beauty, putting the flowers I bought on her desk and turning back to the bed to look over her. Her head is resting on the pillow, her hair spread out like a willow, she flickers those slanted morning eyes until I come into focus and smiles. The sun spray paints features on her face I have never seen before and lights up her eyes.

    I kiss her lips, dry from sleeping, but still soft, and she grabs the back of my head and lures me into her bed. I climb in under the covers. The heat from her body rapidly fills the cold void. She stretches her body and I lay over her, caressing the warm skin beneath her gown with my hands. She grabs the back of my neck again and kisses my lips as I finger through her hair, moving up so she can kiss my Adam's apple.

    After that, I'm in control. I'm totally excited and slide down her body, kissing her navel and making a trail up to her breasts.

    "Good morning," she whispers. I stop to look at her, smile, and we begin to take off each other's clothes.

There is no doubt. We are enjoying senior skip day.

We're both lying on her bed, naked and sweaty, then she gets up and grabs the flowers on her desk, falls back onto the bed smells the sweet petals. I move to my side, placing my elbow on the pillow in preparation for something to say. As I stare into her eyes, she beats me to it.

"Thank you for the flowers, they're great!"

"No problem," I exclaim. "Just found a flower shop…thought it would be okay." For some reason known only to adolescents, I instinctively try to camouflage this unique gesture.

"You were right," she answers happily. "You're so good."

"So, what else did ya wanna do today?" I ask, putting my right arm over her neck.

"I dunno. I kinda just feel like lying around, maybe order a pizza, get some movies, or whatever."

"Right on." I say, lying back onto the pillow as Anna rolls over and places her head onto my arm. "How I love this. With you in my arms, everything seems okay."

"Yeah, I hear that."

CHAPTER 7

❈

We fell asleep, I don't know how long. When I woke up, she was on top of me, whispering softly with each rhythmic movement that she loves me. I fondle her hair, watching as my fingers glide right through the strands without getting caught. I put her bangs behind her ears and reach my head off the pillow to kiss her lips. My hands move from the back of her head down her spine, as the tips of my fingers dig into it making her wiggle back and forth very slowly. She lays her elbows down on the mattress, placing the palms of her hands onto my face, squeezing just a little and kissing me back. I slide my hands up and down her rib cage, they protrude out very slightly.

"That tickles," she says smiling.

She begins kissing my neck, then moves to my shoulders. I feel her tongue slide down the middle of my chest until she does this little spiral thing with her tongue around my belly button. Her nails dig into my chest, I feel my back curve up from the pleasure. I try to look at her, but her hair is pushed forward, covering her face. I grab the back of her arms and pull her back up, wrapping my legs around her waist. She puts her nails into my thighs, starting from the knee cap and pushing down to my private. I smile as my hard-on feels like it's about to explode, it's thumping. I can feel it, up and down, wanting to enter her, and feel that warm comfort that you can only sense in a tub filled with hot water.

Eventually, my legs come apart from her waist, and she puts her legs over mine, sitting on top of my stomach. I feel my penis rub across her pubic hair. She puts one hand on top of my chin, sticking her index finger into my mouth. With her other hand, she grabs my erect penis and slides it into her vagina.

We both let out a moan of satisfaction.

She lays back down on top of me, kissing my neck, as I caress her back. I move my pelvis up and down, slow at first, than faster and faster, until I can feel that tingly feeling in my scrotum, that sense of pent up vexation, that excitement that I can only show Anna physically—until finally, my manhood escapes, and I come inside of her. Then, we hold each other in love, breathing heavy, and laughing.

After our lovemaking, we hop into the shower, kissing and washing each other; no parents were around. We go back to her room wrapped in towels, when the phone rings. Anna rushes to the other room to grab it and leaves me alone. I turn on the TV and flip through channels. Realizing nothing is on, I turn it off and start inspecting her room for something to play with.

Her shelf is filled with little music boxes from all over, probably picked up by her pops while away on business. I start picking them up and turning the knob on each one to create abstract music. Picking up a Chinese musical box with a glass ball and a Buddha sitting cross-legged and smiling, I turn the knob but nothing happens. I turn it over and open the battery compartment. There is something else inside where the batteries should be—a little baggie.

I pull it out, I recognize what it is.

Cocaine.

I look over at the open door to her bedroom, afraid she might be standing there ready to pounce on me.

I refuse to believe such a girl would play with shit like this. I mean, I've done it before, but only on special occasions, and even then…But Anna? Why?

You're supposed to be the one reason to pull me out of this shit, not take me back into it.

I feet hurt more than anything else, and just stare at the package dumbfounded. Then, realizing she's been gone for a while, anger overcomes me. I walk over to my jeans and put the baggie in one of the pockets.

Who the fuck is she talking too?

I tighten the towel around my stomach a little and venture out into the hallway to see what is going on. I hear her voice from the room by the staircase and tiptoe my way along the wall to avoid notice. I don't want to eavesdrop, or be caught eavesdropping for that matter, so I stop and grab a cigarette to stick in my ear, making it look like I was going outside to have a smoke.

Quiet and unseen, I lean against the wall.

I hear only mumbles at first but then, as my ears condition themselves to the distant timbre of her voice, I hear things that piss me off.

"*No, Calvin I don't want to see you anymore*". Pause. "*I don't think that's any of your business*". Pause. "*Listen I gotta' go, I have company over.*"

Company. Is that all I am to her? *What the fuck?* I exclaim to myself.

I feel something different about Anna.

I stare at the empty wall opposite me as my thoughts become undone like a movie reel. Trying to figure out who the fuck this Calvin is, I create a picture in my head of what he might look like trying to talk his way back into Anna's life.

I only manage to see myself walking alone on a cold empty road, filled with sorrow and shame and hate for people.

I know I'm taking this a little too far than I should, so I tell myself this guy must probably be some ex-boyfriend who fucked up and now fully understands what he misses. If Anna really feels the way she's been telling me she feels about us, she'll make the right decision.

"*Yes, Calvin, I found someone else, and I'm happy. So just leave me alone, okay.*"

Pause.

"*We had a good thing going until you tried to get me to sleep with your friends at that fucking party.*"

What? I say to myself. *What the fuck did I just hear? He tried to get her to sleep with his friends. What kind of sick fucker would do a thing like that to Anna?*

I'm still staring at the wall, trying to fathom Anna being fucked by several men, and seeing that look of sorrow on her face…and me not being around to save her! I imagine Calvin as some pimp standing at the foot of her bed, nodding acquiescence with a stupid grin on his face to every man who enters and leaves.

My lips begin to curl under my teeth; my eyes are like sharp arrows. *I don't need to be listening to any of this*, I tell myself. *Leave! Go home! You don't need this shit.*

Yet the thought of walking and not telling her how I feel for her right now forces me to think of another option. I walk back into her room, get dressed and decide to have one of those heart-to-hearts with her when she gets off the phone, which will give me a chance to cool off first.

"*Listen I gotta' get going, I can't talk right now.*" Pause. "*No you can't come over later; I've got plans.*" Pause. "*Okay, listen. I'll tell you if there's any chance tonight. I'll stop by for a second.*"

Pause.

"*All right then.*" Another pause.

As that last sentence leaves her lips, I march back to her room, untangle my clothes from her bed sheets, and call myself a real idiot.

I pull every piece of clothing out from under her comforter and get dressed. Then, throwing my backpack over my shoulder, I proceed towards the front door with loud monster steps, making it known just how mobile my presence is. Anna talks some more and moves around the room by herself, but I make for the staircase.

As I'm placing my hand on the doorknob, Anna cries out from the top of the stairway, "Where are you going?"

I should have kept walking. But, no, like everything in my life, I have to make it complicated, fuck it up, with no clue of what to do with myself next—me, the big planner.

"I'm takin' off," I answer. "Got some other stuff to take care of today."

"Some other…why?" she asks plaintively, the cordless in her hand and the other hand holding on to her hip.

"Come on, don't play dumb. I heard who you were talkin' to. I really don't think it's cool," I reply. I take a momentary pause, trying to regroup my stray thoughts before I explode into a mad rage of jealousy. I wouldn't admit openly to it, but fuck it; if she's gonna' play stupid, I'm gonna' do the same. "Hey…" I say looking at her, "if you got other shit going on today, I don't wanna' interfere or nothin', ya' know."

That's not what I wanted to say.

"Other things are more important to ya' right now, so just give me a call later or somethin'." I turn my back to her and grab the doorknob again, hoping against hope that she'll run down to stop me. To be frank, I don't wanna leave. She's the only reason I like myself. I like myself around her; it shows me the person I can become. She is to me what a winning lottery ticket is to Hector.

She can get me out of my hole. If I leave her now, I'm gonna get blitzed tonight—fuckin' wasted. Do you hear me, God?

I take one slow step at a time.

"Wait a second," Anna says. I hear her steps behind me.

"I gotta' go…" I say, as I turn around with sad dog eyes. She walks down the stairs, grabs my hands, puts them into hers and holds them tight. Staring at her, I notice a white speck in her pupils from the sun behind us that makes me feel warm inside.

"I haven't heard from him in a long time," she whispers. "He just called. There was nothing I could do, ya' know. He just wanted to know how I was doing, that's all."

I don't care, I tell myself and look back at her. But she reassures me, making me feel like I should forget everything that had just happened; not worry and to live in the moment—this moment, right now, where Calvin no longer exists.

But my greediness for love from her needed more reassurance.

"What's this shit about stoppin' by later? I thought it was just gonna' be you and me today?"

"Oh, screw him," she says. "I was just telling him what he wanted to hear, that's all, so I could get back to you." She looks at me like a sad stuffed animal, then down at the floor, placing my hands around her waist and setting hers on my shoulders. "Don't go."

Giving in, I place my head on her shoulder. I allow myself to trust her, having nothing else anyways, and with that, I gently grasp the back of her head and kiss her on the lips. She releases my backpack and kisses me back, telling me how sorry she is.

"Don't worry about it," I say to her.

We were starting the day all over, feeling better now hoping we could just carry on like nothing happened. But, things in my life don't come that easy. That's when the doorbell rings.

CHAPTER 8

❀

His name is Calvin—Anna's ex-boyfriend.

I can see him through the door standing out there on the porch with his dark, straight black hair and silver jewelry shining all over his body, ears, neck, and hands. He's wearing a T-shirt with a beer logo attached to it, which I always found pretty stupid. I mean if you're at a party getting drunk wearing something stupid like that and the cops show up, this tells them right there, 'Hey I'm the drunk one, arrest me'.

Anna takes her hands off me. She opens the door and greets her ex with a confused hello, then, "Why are you here?"

"Well, is everything okay? Are you okay?"

"Yeah," she answers in a slightly sarcastic tone. "Why?"

"Well," he says in a deep bass voice, "When I heard you guys fighting I wanted to come by and make sure you were all right."

"Everything's fine. You'll just make it worse, so go home."

Anna grabs the door and closes it just enough so she can poke her head out, creating a barricade that prevents Calvin and me from exchanging hostile looks.

I walk over to the stairs and take a seat waiting for the door to slam in his face, thinking to myself, *Muthafucker, just leave!*

I hear whispers between them. I decide I don't want to hear any of their conversation because it will just upset me; 'cause if I do, I might just run out there and start some trouble of my own.

Anna's smart. She knows what she's doing—at least that's what I tell myself.

The whispering continues.

Finally, Anna cocks her head back to mouth something to me, her index finger pointing out. *Wait a second*, she is telling me, and then she steps outside and closes the door behind her. At this point, curiosity and insecurity both kick in at the same time. I walk over to the door to pop my ear onto it, hoping to hear whatever I can, but they have already walked off the porch onto the front lawn.

From the front window, I watch them getting angry. He is trying to put his hands on her shoulders, but Anna moves away and just stands there. I don't know what happened to me at this point. I couldn't say what got over me. I guess I'm sick of dealing with problem after problem. I mean, I have enough problems with home and school, I don't want to deal with more problems with Anna. So, I pick up my book bag, go to the living room and walk out through another door. I march through the backyard. All I can think about is why something so simple has to be so difficult. I'm so stupid thinking some girl could change my life. *Fuck him, fuck her!* I don't need this shit in my life.

How I wanted to crack Mr. Ex-boyfriend in his face and confess my love to Anna! But, I think getting smashed sounds more accessible and simple.

I leave, doing what I'm best at, walking outta' the back door.

When I get to the street, he drives by me staring, then turns his car around, drives up to the curb, rolls down his window and yells at me to watch my back, giving me the middle finger. Then he speeds off like a moron back into Anna's neighborhood. I continue to walk, thinking about getting the guys together and dealing with him later, but for now all I want is to get back into my environment and snort this whole bag of coke I took from Anna.

Fuck it! I say to myself and just keep going.

CHAPTER 9

I enter my complex, and the natural smell of exhaust pipes smoking up the air brings me to tears. *I'll never get out of here!*

I'm stuck, failing school, doing drugs, hated by my teachers, my mom, I even hate myself at this point.

I slam my backpack against the side of my apartment building. Snot and tears fly off my face with each swing. I'm yelling at myself, *You're an idiot, a moron, a fuckin' loser!* I smack my hands into the red brick, wishing this wall would collapse over my head, killing me, just to take away the pain.

"Please," I pray to God.

He doesn't answer, and he makes me suffer. He is keeping me alive to live in my own misery and in the misery of others who surround me.

I know there's a good ending to my story, I keep repeating to myself.

I grab my bag and walk to my apartment, telling all the older people I see on the way to fuck off, in my mind. *What are ya' all lookin' at? Go back to your fuckin' soap operas and game shows. Enjoy 'em while ya can, 'cause your time will come, soon!* And I run into my apartment, stomping to my room and jumping into bed with my face in the pillow, giving up and wanting so much to let go…crying…crying…

After sobbing for so long, nothing comes out but dry tears that burn my eyes. I figure the only remedy is the bag in my pocket. I sit up and pull it out, certain that the devil has answered my prayers, not God. I remember how happy I was the last time I did this shit. I felt like I was in heaven. I felt like I could do anything. "My own little muse", I remember hearing this kid call it at a party I was at.

And with the muse in my hand, I grab a chair and head for the bathroom, where I lock the door behind me. I sit myself before the mirror and slowly pull out the bag to lay the shit across the counter, and with a rolled up dollar bill I take the first snort. Then, look at myself in the mirror to make sure there's none on my nose.

I love looking at my eyes when I'm high, watching my pupils grow with each snort. Each pupil becomes one little mouse hole in a big dark cave. I keep snorting and looking in the mirror. More and more.

My eyes begin to lose their color. They become a void, the black center of my universe that I can climb into to escape who I am, but with no idea where I'm going.

Yeah, keep climbing into my pupils, I tell myself. I look back seeing myself staring into the mirror, seeing the shower curtain behind me, the closet door. All this gets smaller and smaller, as I continue walking farther into the tunnel of my eye socket, searching for my piece of mind at peace, having no clue what will happen when I get there.

Where am I going? I ask myself.

I dunno. I'm just high, happy, walking along my own dark yellow brick road.

CHAPTER 10

❀

I feel the sun on my closed eyelids.

VROOM—a breeze floats by and I am shivering, as I lie in the fetal position. I bend towards my feet, looking for the blankets, which I usually shuffle down to the edge of the bed at night. They're not there, probably fell off during the night.

It's so cold. I can't fall back to sleep.

Either I'll have to get up or I'll freeze to death.

VROOM. Cars drive by. Must have left the window open again, I say to myself. Maybe Hec is lying down on the floor next to me and he forgot to close the window when he came in last night.

Another breeze floats across my face.

Lying on my back, I open my eyes and am struck with the bright sunlight. They pierce like lances through my retinas. I close my eyes quickly and cover them with my hands, feeling the tears welling up. Slowly, I pry my eyelids open, but I can still only squint and feel like I have just eaten a lemon. VROOM…VROOM.

"Ya up man?"

"Yeah. Hec?"

"Yup."

I sit up and finally open my eyes, a little more conditioned to the sun's golden rays. It's not the sun that freaks me out. No. It's the place where I'm lying. My hands feel the grass; I'm sitting on the hill next to my apartment, the spot that drops down to form the upper lip of an opening to the creek—the creek of my childhood…The creek that we had all played in when we were younger. While other kids our age were playing handball with their dads before dinner, we used to stare and study down at the creek. This was our father figure. This creek was what made me and my friends into men, or what we thought was the closest thing to it.

I look farther down the path of the creek, watching it flow, remembering the exact place I had jumped across, leaving the fear of falling on the other side. I remember the sheer greatness of extending my step farther than I thought was possible with each jump. When we were chased by foes, it had made our escape easier; and then all we had to do was jump over a gated backyard without flinching.

Sometimes, on rainy days when the father of our times flooded, we would pick other spots to jump from that seemed impossible to clear. But we tested our manhood, and when we fell in, the current would drag us around the complex until we reached the end, under a tunnel filled with rocks. The next challenge wasn't walking in wet-weighted clothes back home, but walking across eroded rocks with sharp ends, green slimy algae on top. If you slipped, the rocks broke your fall and cut up your legs, arms, face, sending you home bleeding, alone, and with none of your friends around to help; that's because if they dared walk you to your ma's house, they'd have to explain what happened, and that meant getting in trouble.

Hec silently looks at the sky, hugging his knees to his chest, creating dreams and images outta' the clouds. I want to ask him how I got here, but I'm afraid I might break his meditation Zen cloud thing. Come to think of it, this is the only time I've ever seen him content. But my curiosity is killing me, like it killed the cat, and if I'm a furry feline, then I know I still have eight more to drop before sinking into the dirt underneath, past those green blades of grass on which I had slept last night.

"Hec, man," I say, rubbing my head, "what the fuck happened last night?"

A smirk rises from his face, but he keeps staring ahead. Finally, he pauses from his cloud thing to look at me with another smirk. "You fuckin' flipped out, dude."

I smile back. "No shit, what did I do?"

"Man, when I snuck into your crib through the window, I found your ass half-naked in the closet, swimming around in your clothes."

We both laugh. "Get the hell outta' here!"

"Naw, man, I'm serious. Your stupid ass had all your clothes that were on hangers scattered across the floor like flotsam on a polluted body of water, with your ass in the middle doin' the back stroke like a dolphin, so I picked your ass up and sat you against the wall telling you to chill out for a sec. If you don't believe me, look at your belly, man, you got carpet burn all over."

I lift up my shirt. There were big welts across my stomach and chest. I watch them shrink and expand with every breath of laughter.

"So, yeah," Hec continues, "after I put your ass in the corner, I went to take a piss and found what you been doin'. Luckily, you got a good friend like me, 'cause I cleaned up the mess before your mom found it. Then I grabbed you, threw ya' outta' the window and we hung out under a bridge."

I try, but I can't remember a thing. All I know is that he wasn't pulling my leg.

"How did you clean up the mess?" I ask. "Did you use a towel or your nose, you schmuck?"

"Whatcha think, tough guy? You were saying some messed up shit too, man. About living around here and about Anna and shit…"

I stop laughing. Now I remember what had happened the night before. Standing up and stretching, I tell Hec how I ruined it with Anna—or how she ruined it—and about how I just walked away.

"Aw…what the fuck ya' bitchin' about man? There's other fish in the sea.", he proclaims.

"Whaddya mean, Hec? You don't mean around these parts? I know you're not talkin' about this fuckin' dirt pool in front of us, are ya? The only thing I'll find in this toilet-infested dog bowl is a sea creature with three arms talkin' gibberish and wantin' me ta touch her wet fins." As I squat back down, Hec looks at me funny with a confused expression.

"Man, you're messed up. Just keep puttin' that shit up your nose. I think it's makin' ya' smarter."

"Aw…," I say, "fuck off."

We both laugh and knock each other around, wrestling, not having a care in the world, throwing rocks into our future; looking for the answer to our prayers from big daddy creek, jumping across, proclaiming our dreams and how they'll happen if we make it across; doing what any kid our age would with nothing better to do: sit around and dream.

After a few more hours of hanging around, I finally make it back to my apartment. Jaw sore from too much laughing, leg sore from jumping, and brain fuzzy from too much coke. Suddenly, I feel alone and sad. It usually happens this way when reality sinks back in. One moment, I'm feeling on top of the world, the sun above me like a light bulb filled with dreams and ideas that may happen some day; the next moment, well, the sun drifts away to become inspiration for some other schmuck. That's when the darkness hits me. It just gets too gloomy. Shadows reappear and I sneer at all the hopes I harbored only a minute ago.

I'm standing in my living room looking out the window. I long for the sun to shine its light on me. I hope the sun will make me happy again. I'll take it if it comes for only a few more seconds.

But I'm all alone with a note from my mom. She's out doing who knows what, returning whenever with whomever. All I know is I'd better be gone before she returns, knowing she'll lay into me big time for not coming home last night, and that's the type of shit I don't wanna deal with right now, with Anna gone and no drugs to make me happy.

I stand by the dinner table, since it was a hand-me down from another tenant across the hall who was moving out to live in a house with her new husband. That's how things get schlepped around here, like family heirlooms passed from one poor person to the next.

The phone rings. Maybe it's the answer, my small piece of happiness until the next one appears. I pick it up.

"Hello."

"Hey, hey, hey, Sol. Guess who?"

This will do for now.

CHAPTER 11

❁

I met Adam at a party a couple months back. The guys and I were helping Jug sell some shit to the rich kids—you know the type: on the school sport teams, looking for weekend gigs, alcohol, drugs, and disoriented girls. Pretty sick but they had money. I had just gone through the medicine cabinets looking for cough medicine to go with a couple tabs of acid I had gotten off of Jug. Finding what I needed, I went to raid the fridge and grabbed a carton of orange juice for a chaser. Behind me, Adam asked me to pass him a beer. I put one in his hand and closed the fridge.

"Why aren't you drinking, man?" he inquired.

I heard some talk around school of some kids working as narcs for the cops, especially those rich kids who get busted because of their small habits, and then give up everything to keep their asses out of jail. So I was a little defensive. I found his question kind of curious.

"Why do you care?" I asked.

"Oh, I dunno. Just askin', that's all."

I gave him half a smirk and turned around to face him.

"So, you with those kids in the garage?" he wanted to know.

I shook my head, "Naw", and I walked away, going to the garage with friends I denied knowing, preparing to eat acid and drink cough medicine with OJ on the side.

As the night progressed, Adam came out to the garage and started chatting with us about other kids he knew who had parties every weekend. He told Jug how he could make some loot. All he wanted for the info was a little of whatever Jug made that night.

"Of course." Jug agreed.

Since then, Adam's been more or less part of our crew, even coming out to the apartments and partying with us. But that's all he really is: a party friend, someone to kick it with here and there when nothing else is happening.

We became good enough friends that he calls me now, although when he did for the first time, I was still kind of surprised.

"What's happenin', Adam?"

"Not too much, man. Just hangin' out-ya know?"

"Yeah," I answer.

"So what's your plans for tonight?"

"Nothin', man, not feelin' too well, ya know, had a rough night."

"Yeah, man, I hear that. Did ya skip school, too?"

"Yeah. Hung out with Anna, but that didn't go too well. I'm not sure but I think we broke up."

"I heard about that shit, man," he says, which caught my attention.

"How did you find out?"

"I saw her last night at a party, lookin' a little gloomy with some dude, and I talked to her for a minute."

"Really?" I say surprised. "What did you say?"

"Well, when I didn't see ya around, I asked her where you were at, and she told me you just left without saying anything."

"Did she tell you why I left?" I ask, starting to get pissed.

"Yeah, and I don't blame you man, but deal with that shit later. I knew you would be feelin' a little glum. That's why I'm callin', I want you to come out with me tonight. I got some shit happenin' that'll take your mind off things."

"Cool," I answer enthusiastically.

"Some kids and me are goin' to a carnival and then a party in the next town over."

"You think Anna will be there?" I wonder out loud.

"I dunno," he replies. "I doubt it. I don't think she knows these kids, but who cares man. There's gonna be so many girls at this party tonight!"

"Yeah, I know," I say in frustration. "I just don't think I'm up for being around a bunch of kids tonight."

"Oh, fuck that," Adam utters into the phone. "The kids we're goin' to the carnival with heard of you…and a couple girls in particular even told me to bring you, 'cause they want to meecha!"

"Yeah?"

"Yeah, so don't say another word. I'll be over in a little bit to pick you up."

"All right," I answer.

I'm sitting outside our apartment, waiting for Adam to come and scoop me up; the sun is starting to set. Three cars pull into our lot and park right next to each other; Adam comes out of one of the rides and walks towards me, I don't get up.

"Hey, kid, what's happenin'?" he says as he smacks my hand.

"Not too much, ya know. So, what are we doin' first?" I ask looking past Adam to see who is in the other cars.

"We're gonna go to a carnival first, maybe do a little somethin' before we hop on the rides…then go to the party."

"Cool," I reply with a smirk still trying to figure out who's in the other cars.

"You ready man?"

I nod my head and rise to walk behind Adam, who opens the driver's side door of his car. Before I walk up to his ride, he stops me. "Hey, man, you're not riding with me. You're in that car," he says, pointing to the Explorer next to his. I look over and see three girls staring at me with smiles.

"Okay," I say and walk over to the Explorer. I open the back passenger side door. "Hi. Adam said I should ride with you guys?"

The driver smiles with red lipstick and says, "No problem, hop in." We exchange a few glances and nods of the head as we drive out of the complex and scream down the road. The two girls in front are talking with each other and playing loud music. The girl next to me is silent, just looking ahead. Nobody's saying a word to me. I don't even know their names, but I do know they're talking about me. The two girls up front keep looking back at me with smiles, but the music's so loud I can't hear what their saying.

We stop at a red light, and the driver turns down the music, looking back at me. "So your name's Solomon, right?"

"Yeah," I answer. "What's your names?"

"Well, I'm Samantha," says the driver. "This is Nikki," who twists around from the front seat and shakes my hand. "And that back there is Claudia," who just turns her head and nods. The light turns green and Samantha turns the music back up, both girls up front are bopping around to the music, while Claudia just keeps staring ahead. Most of the ride was silent, no talking, just grooving to the music, and watching the girls up front look back at me with smiles.

As the sun sets, we enter the parking lot of a church, which I guess every year holds a fundraiser for the regular worshippers. We all get out of the cars and huddle around the back of the Explorer. I watch everyone else squeeze close together, as Adam pulls out a bag of joints, hands one to me to light up and a couple more to the others.

Samantha and Nikki box me in, Samantha holding onto my left arm as I puff away on the joint, passing it to Nikki, who in turn passes it to the next. Everyone's getting high, holding their own conversation to the person next to them. Adam talks back and forth, and quickly glances back at me, smiling as both girls next to me press their breasts against my arms. Nikki places her hand on my chest and leans over me to talk to Samantha, both smelling like some fruity body wash and telling each other how cute I am.

I stand in the middle, silent, puffing away on whatever gets passed to me.

The high kicks in as we walk towards the entrance, and I'm being led by Samantha and Nikki feeling like a six-year-old boy. The neon light gleaming overhead shocks my pupils and propels my mind to euphoric heights. I remember when my mother took me to festivals and being caught under all the bright lights and the jubilation of the moment. She would hold my hand, knowing well that I could venture off at any second to find my own glory in rolling skee balls and Ferris wheels. Back then, I needed to see everything all at once, and if I didn't I was devastated.

Some of those rides were downright dangerous. *One day*, I would say to myself, *I'll ride these big monsters the whole way through and finish off the night with an elephant ear.* The more I went to carnivals with friends over the years, the less excitement I had, until the disco lights and teddy bear games were nothing more than a half-hour TV show that was on for five days straight.

But tonight we have drugs to recapture that first level of excitement. They will boost my senses and lift small little bumps on my arms. And instead of my mom holding my hand towards some inchoate happiness, I have two girls on either side to recreate my six-year-old experience. And I don't even have to win them a stuffed animal.

Samantha and Nikki drag me ahead of everyone else. At this point, I can't even tell if I'm walking; they cling to me like leeches, lifting me high. I feel like I'm levitating across the dirt ground . We hop in line for a ride, but I'm too fucked up to remember what this huge circular mass in front of me is called. It lights up in green and yellow and expands across the sky, blue and red, continuously.

The girls laugh—at what, I have no clue. But I'm laughing, too, smiling big, looking around the carnival and at the fat bearded man taking our tickets. I see children smothering their faces in cotton candy. Other teenagers stand around peeping out others; boys looking at girls, exchanging glances, smiling; older people handing out pamphlets to the walkers-by with, *Keep your faith in God!*

I float up to a caged box and watch the girls laugh, rubbing my cheeks, because they're getting so stiff from the content look on my face that feels like a plastic doll with a happy expression. The bearded man pushes the button and yells, "Ya'll ready to fly on the Ferris wheel?"

"That's what it's called!" I yell out, my jaw laughing mechanically, my eyes wide as doorknobs. We jerk forward and begin moving slowly up. The girls are rubbing against my body, but as I watch all the lights change colors my mind is set on cotton candy. I want to buy the biggest roll on a stick and I don't care how much it costs. But climbing higher and higher starts to make me nervous.

I look over at Samantha. Her blonde long hair is flying around her head like a sail, I grab at it and hit her tufts to keep them moving. She draws closer to me and kisses me on the lips. I feel the hairs on the back of my neck grow a couple inches. My hands are all over both girls; their hands all over me like a full body massage. Then the three of us tilt our heads back and climb higher and higher, our hands rubbing each others body harder and harder.

I'm gripped by one blinking star in the sky. Its white light dims then brightens again.

I must be on my way to heaven.

Is it possible? Has this church finally achieved the impossible, building the Tower of Babel. Can we see heaven from here?

Sure, says the star, blinking as it speaks to me. "Come on up, Solomon."

"I'm a bird," I yell out, extending my arms as if they were wings. The two girls join me and extend their arms.

The breeze gets cooler and stronger as we reach our stellar height. The sky darker except for the stars, mine in particular, which beams brighter. I hear screams of joy coming from other caged souls and see clouds in the dark skies.

Samantha and Nikki kiss my cheek like angels.

Floating, I unlock the cage and close my eyes. I fly ever higher into the sky.

Am I…almost…there star?

Yes, my star answers, *just a little more.* I look down and see everything as small specks of dust-like looking at the stars from the ground. I smile and go on flying through heaven.

I decide to name that star Anna. Then, closing my eyes, I lie back to enjoy the ride.

CHAPTER 12

We're here Sol, wake up!

I shuffle around in my seat to get a look around, having no clue how I got back in the car with the girls. The music's low and nice, my seat warm, the girls quiet. I sit up.

"How long have I been out?"

"Since we got back in the car," one of them answers.

After looking around some more, I realize we're in a neighborhood. I could tell from the lamp posts illuminating the houses. I don't say a word. I'm not even gonna ask about the carnival or what happened. If I tell them I don't remember shit, they might get mad. I rub my head trying to recall what happened after the Ferris wheel, but nothing comes to. All I recall was my way up to heaven, and then I think: *Did I make it there?*

I look at Claudia. Her blank silent stare forward triggers a little chuckle in me.

When we step out of the car, Samantha and Nikki walk arm in arm towards the house, leaving Claudia and me alone. At the front porch, the door opens up and fifty pairs of shoes strewn around the entrance to greet us. We have to walk around them, but I just follow Samantha and Nikki, realizing I don't know a single soul at this party.

There are people in every room we pass by. Kids everywhere. We get to the living room. Everyone there is carrying a beer and talking loudly over the music. The coffee table is filled with empty beer cans, bags of chips, and cigarette butts, bodies lying around the family room, some sick from too much drinking, others making out in the only privacy they could find, a secluded corner behind the dining room table.

I end up losing Samantha and Nikki somewhere between the talking bodies in the hallway and the voyeurs watching a guy puke up a lung in the toilet. I make my way to the kitchen, wondering whose house this is. And where's Adam? Were Jug and the guys gonna make it out?

I walk into the kitchen, kegs stuck in the corner next to the fridge. Mom-and-dad's liquor cabinet broken open and spread across the kitchen counter like a deck of cards at a poker game. I stand looking at everyone, feeling a little awkward because I know no one and my high is starting to come down. I turn towards the bottles to choose a fifth of Jack Daniels as a pick-me-up for now. All I need is a nice quiet place in seclusion.

I ponder this as I grab the bottle without anyone seeing me, sticking it under my shirt and walking nonchalantly out of the kitchen and back into the hallway looking for a place to hide out. *I just wanna get drunk and think about Anna,* I mumble.

I refuse to go upstairs, knowing that behind those closed doors will be kids and wild sex. Maybe I should just sit outside. I start walking towards what I think is the back door, open it and find the laundry room. The washer and dryer sit next to one another in silence, in the dark, with only the moon for a light. I recall Hec telling me once that if the moon is halfway out, turn your head to the side and it will be smiling at you. With that thought, I smile back. I've found my quiet place to hide.

Alone again.

I drag myself down across the wall to the tiled floor, twisting the cap off the bottle and taking a quick slug, like a coffee drinker would at a coffee shop.

But then I put the bottle down on the floor and plump my head into the palms of my hands. Nothing will make me as happy as I was at the carnival, or the creek earlier today. Why can't I be like other people my age? I think of Adam and how he goes to school every day, talks to his parents, pretty much leads a normal life.

I wish I could be like Beaver Cleaver. What the fuck does he have to worry about? That dude has two parents that love him, dinner every night, friends to hang out with; he can do fun things like play baseball and read comic books. I wish I had that…normal life, the girl that loves me, a future. Anything to get me away from here. I want to go some place different, see new things, wake up in silence.

I pray for an answer, or a gunshot wound to the chest, just so I could sit in the hospital undisturbed for a while and not have to be around anything.

Suddenly a flame ignites on the side of the washer. Am I tripping? I take another swig from the bottle.

"Ya wanna hit?" a voice says from behind me.

"What?" I ask, getting off the floor to draw closer to whoever is there.

"I'll share this with ya…if you share that bottle with me." Light-headed from rising too quickly, I see a girl sitting down and about to smoke a joint. She is looking at the same moon I was contemplating. I slog a little closer to her, until the moon's white light illuminates her face. It's Claudia, the silent one who didn't say a single word to me the whole ride. I sit down next to her, plop the bottle between us and grab the joint from her fingers. "Thanks," I say, puffing away.

Inhaling the smoke, I ask in a deep voice, "So what are you doing here by yourself?" I blow smoke out and pass the joint back to her.

"I dunno," she says as she takes her first toke. "Guess I'm not much of a people person."

"Yeah, I hear that. I wanted to sit outside somewhere…that's what I thought this door led too," pointing to the door with the joint in hand.

"Then, when ya think you're alone, someone is peering at you from behind the washer," she softly chuckles.

"No shit," I exclaim, thinking that this might be my moment of happiness for the time being.

"Are you always that quiet?" I ask, grabbing the bottle by the neck and handing it to her for a first swig.

"Naw, not really. Just that today was no good. I wasn't in the mood to be sociable…Wow that burns!" She quickly puts the bottle down.

"I know it's some strong shit isn't it?"

She nods her head, agreeing.

"Why was today a bad day?"

"Well, I found out my boyfriend was cheating on me with one of my friends."

"Wow that sucks."

I feel her pain and hand the bottle back to her, and while she's sipping I tell her about Anna and what happened yesterday.

"Isn't that a coincidence?"

We stare at each other. It wasn't even one of those romantic looks, but a look of sorrow, of understanding. We both nod our heads in agreement, realizing we can relate to each other. And as we finished the joint, we continue drinking, talking about the ones who have hurt us, comparing stories, giving each other insight, opinions on the matter. I ask her about women. "What should I do?"

"Well, I think you should tell her what you were thinking, explain your side before jumping to conclusions, ya know. Maybe she feels the same way. You don't know until you ask."

I shake my head, taking her advice to heart and telling myself what I'm gonna do tomorrow. *Call her up*, I think, *and just explain everything; she'll understand.*

I play the conversation over in my head, sipping the bottle.

Anna, I don't know what got over me. I'm sorry for leaving. It was just seeing you talking with your ex-boyfriend and everything got me a little jealous.

I understand Solomon, don't worry, him and I are over. He means nothing to me, nothing at all. You're the one I love, your the one who makes me happy. I'm sorry. I'm sorry you that had to happen our special day we had planned. Nothing like that will ever happen again.

You're the best Anna. I love you.

I love you too Solomon.

This brings a small ray of light.

Claudia and I continue talking, leaving relationships on the back burner and going on to different things, like who we are. I see that not all rich kids have everything. And when she looks at my life she finds it limitless, not as immobile as I thought.

The bottle disappears quickly into our stomachs, but we aren't through talking. I want to sit here all night, and she wants the same, but not without more to drink. "Let's put this on pause," I say emphatically, "until I find another bottle, then we can continue."

"Sounds good," she says, shaking her head in agreement. I get up and almost flop back down on the ground from the sudden head rush, which blocks my vision and increases my high. "I think someone needs a wheel chair," she says, laughing.

"Oh, you think that's funny, do ya?"

Slowly my vision returns and my head clears. I walk over and open the door, turning my head to the side and covering up my eyes with my hands to block the white lights illuminating the hallway. I look back at Claudia, who stands up and stretches. I turn back to the hallway, taking a few steps out the utility room. Then, I see a couple of guys walk towards me.

"What the fuck is this?" A kid says from across the hall, standing with the others. I look over at him and shrug my head thinking he isn't speaking to me. But, when I look back, Claudia is looking over my shoulder with a shocked expression on her face. This tells me he's talking to us. Before I can turn my head back towards the hallway, I feel my body shoved into the doorway. Then, I'm grabbed by my shirt and pushed into a wall. The impact of my back against the dry wall creates this loud bang and shakes the house. Everyone falls silent. The music suddenly is turned down low, and I can hear feet shuffle through the house trying to locate the commotion.

I hear Claudia yell at the guy, telling him to get his hands off me. But he doesn't listen, just holds onto my shirt with one hand and pins me to the wall, all the while looking over his shoulder at Claudia.

"What the fuck are ya doing?" she yells, walking towards us and getting in his face.

"What the fuck do ya mean? I should be asking you that!" he says loudly, tightening his grip on my shirt.

"Dan, just leave him alone."

"Naw, fuck that, not till you tell me what you guys were doin' in there?"

"It's none of your business," she shouts, sending echoes across the hallway, bringing groups of people from out the woodwork to see what's happening.

Dan, I guess is his name, turns his attention back on me, his hands gripping my shirt. "What the fuck were you guys doin, huh?" My eyes widen from shock, my heart pumping like crazy. I can't think straight from the Jack Daniels and the pot, all I can do is stare at him, look into his piercing eyes, at his leather jacket, and dirty shoes; while his two friends stare at me from either side. The only thought racing through my mind is to act tough, and hope, pray to God that Hec and Jug are around to help me out.

The whole house is crunched into this one hallway. Some kids whisper into each other's ears and stare, others yell at us from the back of the house to fight.

Hit him!

He continues to stare at me, clenching his fists tighter on my shirt and nudging me into the wall awaiting his answer. Claudia begins to speak up, allowing my tough guy routine to be put on hold for a moment. Dan, probably the guy that's been cheating on her, the one she was talking about earlier, lets go of me and starts speaking to Claudia.

"What the fuck were you two doing in there?"

"Nothing, just talkin'. That was it, and what do you care? I'm not your girlfriend anymore." They continue to argue, leaving me trapped against a wall, having to listen to all this bullshit.

"Hey, man," I speak out. "We weren't doin' anything. Just bullshittin, ya know."

He turns to me and gets right into my face. "Did I ask you, asshole?" I can smell his beer breath under my lip. His two friends are getting closer to us.

"Oh, this is fucking stupid," Claudia says from behind. "I'm outta here."

Dan and I both turn our heads and watch her walk away through the crowd of people. Just as she passes the front door, I see Anna standing to the side, trying to look above the heads to see what's happening. My vision fixed on her, I see a cream-colored face. Everything else around me suddenly vanishes, like a closing scene for a movie. I only see her.

The crowd is yelling for us to fight. But I can't see Dan giving me his cold stare, and can't think of my pain as these three guys pound my head to the pulp. I keep looking at her, remembering how beautiful she was naked, thinking about that light that struck her skin the day we met.

Everything's gonna be okay, I say to myself. It's as if she is telling it to me herself. I need to go to her, tell her I'm sorry.

Then, she sees me. She gazes right into my eyes, and for a moment I think I see a smile, which quickly vanishes as she shakes her head in disappointment and walks out the front door, her ex following right behind her, looking over at me and yelling loudly, "Fuck him up!"

With Anna gone everything comes back, the noise from the others, the beer breath on Dan, his tight grip against my chest, the airy feeling in my head from being drunk and high, the room beginning to spin, adrenaline kicking in from the anger welling up inside me. And then my mind yells at me to go to her. This is your only chance to make things right.

I pry loose Dan's grip to run towards the door, but he won't loosen up and just smacks me across the face. My head bangs against the wall with a loud thud. Pain shoots through my body and heats my face into a hot ember. I feel a tingle spread across my jaw. That's when I lose it. I jump up and easily loosen his grip on my shirt, and he lets go. I grab his coat and throw him into the wall. Everything hanging falls down and shatters on the floor. As he shakes off the sudden pain from his neck, his face turns red and he lunges at me. But before he can get to me, I grab a beer bottle out of one of his friend's hands and swing it, catching his head and shattering the glass and suds across his face. He drops to the ground, knocked out cold, and blood oozing out of his head. Everyone close by freezes, not saying a word. I drop the rest of the bottle on the ground and run across the hallway towards the front door, everyone moving out of my way.

Passing one of the front windows, I see Anna and that asshole, out front getting into his car. I rip open the front door and run towards her. "Wait!" I yell, running across the front lawn. Anna stops before getting into the car and stands with her arms folded waiting for me to speak.

"Don't go," I tell her. "I need you. I'm sorry for just leaving. I thought you didn't want me there."

"Let's go, Anna," her ex says from the driver's side.

"Shut up," I yell back, pointing my finger menacingly at him. "Don't listen to this guy, Anna. I love you, and I know you love me, don't do this. You're all I got."

Anna just stares at me. She sees that I'm serious, her face starting to soften. I'm getting to her, she's gotta know I'm for real. I put my hands out, wanting for her to take them. I hear kids from behind yelling and screaming about what I did.

"Don't pay attention to them," I shout to her.

She's looking over my shoulder, listening to what everybody's saying. Her ex yells for me to get away from the car. I hear sirens in the distance. Anna's eyes are puffing up, my hands still extended forward. People begin filling up the front lawn; others are heard inside yelling about the bloody Dan in the hallway. Anna looks at me, the moon reflecting from her eyes.

"I'm sorry, Sol," she says softly. "It's through." She gets into the car, but before closing it, she says. "I don't know what you're talking about anyways, we only went out for a couple months," then slams the door, her ex turning the car on and speeding off.

I drop to my knees; hands still extended and start to cry at the top of my lungs, "*Nooo*," looking up at the sky. "*You're all I got!*"

I grab the grass and start pulling it out, failing to understand why she would say this. My heart pounds against my chest; I just want to cut it out to make it stop. It hurts. My eardrums throb. I hear kids' voices and sirens come in and out over the throbbing in my ears. I go on crying and calling out her name aloud.

She was all I had; I was going to change…I was going to be happy. And then, in my head, I envision myself once again holding her in my arms. We smile at each other, walking down an aisle. I'm coming home where we live. I open the front door and there she is. I kiss her passionately on the lips.

"*I love you Sol*," she whispers.

"*I love you too*," I answer.

From behind me I hear, "*You muthafucker!*" Then "WHACK" everything goes black, and I am walking down that same dark tunnel as before when I was doing coke in my bathroom.

Where am I going this time?

I don't know...Just keep walking...

CHAPTER 13

I have one day. One day to say goodbye to my friends. One day to try and get a hold of Anna to say farewell. One day to walk along a street by myself.

That's what the judge gave me, one day to say good-bye to my loved ones before I leave for six months of drug rehab. This was a lenient sentence; I was young with no prior record. But I was told if I mess this up, I'd go away to a detention center for a longer time. The cop who cracked me across the back of the head was real pissed. During the case, I would look over my shoulder, and see him staring at me with a mean ass face, all dressed up in uniform with his mirror reflected sunglasses probably hoping that if he came dressed up, showing the court he was a law man like themselves, they would throw the book at me. Give me a sentence worth ten teens, closing the light of day from my eyes for years.

When he first heard the sentence, his hands went up in the air, and they came down smacking the oak bench, creating a loud disturbance. He wanted everyone in the court room to recognize his rage. When the judge cracked his gavel down that's when everyone started to walk out of the courtroom except that cop. He walks over to me and grabs me by the arm. I watch my eyes become the size of grapefruits in his glasses.

"I'll be lookin for you punk," he whispers in my ear. "I'm gonna make sure you screw up in rehab cause I want you to go to that detention center. I know a lot of officers there that owe me favors, and they love fresh meat, especially one as cute as you if ya catch my drift asshole."

He throws my arm off to the side and stands for a second staring at me. Then, he cracks a smile from the side of his lips and walks outta the courtroom.

He has such a hard on for me cause it is his son that is now in the hospital. Yep, his son is the one I knocked out with the bottle.

At home, I run to the phone to call Anna, but I get an answering machine and leave her a message, without going into much detail. I only say that today is my last day before I leave for a six month trip. After, I hang up the phone and go to my room to grab the rest of my money, deciding the best thing for me right now is to get fucking wasted. I pull out one of the books from my shelf and pocket the remaining cash, put the book back, and walk out. Before I open the front door, my mom grabs my arm.

"You're so stupid. What's the matta with ya?"

"I don't know," I reply trying to get her to loosen her grip.

"You know you're lucky. And I'm glad you're going away 'cause you'll need the discipline," she says with beady bloodshot eyes.

"Mom just leave me alone, okay. I'll be back later!"

"What are you, stupid? Don't be going back out there to hang out with those stupid friends of yours. You'll just get into more trouble!"

"Don't worry," I yell. "I'll be back in a little bit!"

"You're gonna die, Solomon! You're gonna die very soon!" She hollers at me.

I loosen her grip from my arm and run out the front door, hearing her whimper as she shuts the door. I punch the building door open and run out, trying to hold in my tears, feeling the heavy weight of guilt. I run as fast as I can over to Hector's, hoping to death he's home. I knock on the door and look over my shoulder watching as the man living next door walks past me, shaking his head like he knows what just happened to me at the courthouse. Hec opens the door and I push myself in, slamming the door behind me. I look into the peephole to see if anyone else is around.

"Yo, kid, what the fuck is wrong with you?"

"I don't know, man, it was like that fucking old guy next door knows what happened to me. He was looking at me, shaking his head and shit."

"Oh, you talkin' about your court case today, how'd that go?" he asks going over to the couch.

"Shitty," I reply, still looking out the peephole.

"Man chill the fuck out. Ain't no old man gonna be fuckin' with you."

Seeing no one in the hallway, I walk over to the recliner and take a seat.

"So what did they give ya?"

"Six months in drug rehab," I say.

"No shit, you gonna go?"

"Whaddya mean am I gonna go? Of course! I got no choice."

"Well, chill out for a minute all right? Hit this shit," Hec says, as he passes a lit joint my way.

I take a hit and make it a long one, hoping I'll overdose and die. I feel the smoke in my lungs and let it out calmly. It hits me a little and I start to cool down.

"Man, if I was in your situation, I would fuckin' run. There's no way I'm getting locked up. Shit, I'd just run to my cousin's place in the big city and hide out," Hec says as he hits the joint.

"Yeah, but if you ever got busted for anything, there'll probably be a warrant. Then you'll be fucked even more," I reply.

"Naw, them pigs wouldn't be able to catch me."

"Whatever, man." I get up from the recliner and grab the phone.

"So when do you leave?"

"Tomorrow."

"That fuckin' soon? Where am I gonna stay when you're gone?"

"I don't know, Hec. Stay down by the creek."

I dial Anna's number, but again I get the machine.

"Fuck! Where is she?"

"Who?"

"Anna."

"Fuck if I know. Hey man, fuck her. She screwed you man, and now you're trying to get hold of her? Man, you're stupid. Why don't you just chill out and get fucked up for the last time."

I walk back to the recliner and take a seat, double-toking the joint to cool out a little more. Hec is leaning deep into the couch all messed up. I start to feel angry that I can't get a hold of Anna, the girl I'm in love with. I start to think about where she is, ideas forming in my head about whom she's with. I start pounding my fists against the arms of the recliner as my ideas turn sexual, but without me in the picture.

"I'm fucked," I whisper to myself as I stare ahead projecting my thoughts onto the carpet. "Fuck it!"

Looking into my future, I see myself locked up without anyone around for six months; hanging out with sober geeks praying or whatever the hell they do, and I know they'll be trying to turn me against my friends. They'll be trying to brainwash me like they did to some other kids I know. I remember a while back, before school started, I was hanging out in the hall when an old friend of mine, Allen, he walked up to me and asked me if I wanted to go to a meeting with him. He had gone to rehab.

"What, an AA meeting?" I remember asking, laughing in his face.

"Yeah, man. What you're doin' right now isn't too healthy. You need to smarten up."

I pretty much told him to fuck off, thinking back about how he used to hangout with us and get high all the time. When he came back from rehab, he started saying how he wasn't allowed to hang out with us anymore, and that he found God and good people. Apart from all that, just the way he looked in general after returning gave me a chill. He used to be hyperactive, and when he got wasted, he was funny as all hell. Now he's a lush, serious all the time, always thanking and being humble, as he called it. I never understood the shit and I wasn't about to. He reminds me of a zombie, someone dead, something I don't want to become.

My high starts to take off, and when that happens I usually start to hallucinate. Right now wouldn't be a good time for that, though, seeing I'm not in the best of moods, plus with a bump the size of the Himalayas on the back of my brain doesn't help. I really wish I were able to fly off to heaven when I was on that Ferris wheel.

I start to drift off and to stare at some inanimate object for God knows how long, thinking only about how I wouldn't be able to see Anna; about how I haven't seen her, kissed her, touched her in a few days. It feels like a year.

I rub my head to get that tingly feeling I could absorb in my brain. When I open my eyes, I see spots for a few seconds and decide against going to rehab. *Fuck it*, I think. Being a fugitive is better. The big city is a nice hide out. I've been through enough punishment without my Anna; I'm not going through any more.

"Hec, hey, do you think your cousin will let us stay with him?"

"Yeah, kid," he mumbles, his head dropping for a second before he picks it back up and turns to me with half-opened eyes. Smiling, he says. "He'll be down."

"Well, call him up," I say excitedly, throwing the cordless phone to the cushion next to him.

"Naw, man...can't."

"Why not?"

"'Cause he don't got no phone."

"Then, how do we get hold of him?" I ask, annoyed and hoping this wasn't bullshit.

"We just...show up."

CHAPTER 14

❀

Hec and I go through his mom's jewelry. Most of it is fake, except a couple rings that his dad gave her back in the seventies.
Vintage stuff. That's what the pawn guy calls it.
We also decide to take the blender, the toaster, a couple pairs of earrings, a cheap Polaroid camera, a couple dirty movies I find under Hector's bed, a lamp from one of the end tables that had some glowing lava thing happening on the base, a broken beta player, an old Sega with two games, and finally Hector's black and white ten inch TV.
The living room becomes a mountain of junk and now we have to figure out how to haul all this stuff to the pawn shop. Hec thinks we should walk to the grocery store and steal a shopping cart from the parking lot.
"I'm game," I say.
As we get to the grocery store, we grab a cart and begin running with it down the sidewalk along a main, busy road. Hec decides to get in and I push him around, laughing and scaring the day lights outta him as I run faster down the sidewalk. Hec's got his fingers entangled into the cart hoping it doesn't tip.

"Don't worry, I'm a professional," I holler as I get ready to run with the cart across the middle of the intersection with Hector still in it.

I have the cart at a pretty decent speed now; I can't slow it down to look both ways before crossing the street. I see a patch of grass I have to go over and a curb I have to jump.

I run as fast as I can down the sidewalk, then jump up and put my feet on the bottom of the cart, usually where people put their dog food, and we fly across the patch of grass with Hector yelling, "OH SHIT!"

We get a couple inches of air off the curb and we land smack dab on the yellow line of a two lane intersection. Hec drops his head down and covers it with his hands, as I first look to the left watching all the traffic come at me, honking their horns and slamming on their brakes. Hector without looking throws his twelve ounce bottle of pop from behind him and I watch as it smacks a lady in a convertible right smack dab on her head.

"You little fuckers," I hear her say as we get to the other side of the solid yellow line in the street.

As the cars come at us from the right, they slam on their brakes and holler. I forget to pop a wheelie, as we fly across, before hitting the curb. The front two wheels of the cart smack into the concrete, sling-shooting me from the back of the cart to the sidewalk. When I look over at Hector, I see that he never got outta the cart; it's just rolling in circles with him still in it. I run over to him, and see, after flipping the cart to its side, that he's pretty banged up. With him still in it, I flip the cart back on its wheels and run with it again down the sidewalk. This time with a limp in my leg to get outta sight before the people in their cars come running out to kick our ass.

"You're an asshole," Hector mumbles with his hands over his forehead barely conscious.

At the pawnshop, the guy offers us two hundred dollars for all our junk. I look over at Hector who's about to say, "We'll take it". But, I cover up his mouth and ask if we could get a little better price?

"Well, I dunno youngsters. I only get a few of your kind in here…And hey I'm always willin to help the less fortunate, but youse gots to understand; I sometimes have ta consider the fact that youse all ain't angels, and some of this shit might be hot. Know what I'm sayin'?"

"Fine we'll take it," I say holding out my hand.

We're at the bus station. I'm in line buying tickets, while Hec slouches with his ass half off the hard chair, trying to get some shut eye. I think he's on something else or at least he should be after the spill we took from the shopping cart incident. My high to ease the pain from the limp in my leg has been gone for a little while now, and I'm just a little tired from coming down. But, Hec is almost completely out, probably high from the white powder he took from my bathroom the other night.

Smelling like mothballs, the old lady in front of me finally leaves after asking countless questions in her little old lady voice—*How do you get to my bus? Where is the bus? I take a left there, then What?*

I finally get up front. The black lady at the counter asks me where I'm going?

"To the big city. How much is it for two tickets?"

"Fifty dollars."

"I'll take 'em."

I show her the fifty, but I really give her a twenty. A con man's trick I perfected after learning it from Jug's dad one night while partying at his house. What you do, is take the bill and you fold it the long way. Then, again until you make it into a "W". You stick the middle part of the "W" in between your fingers, making sure the ends of the bill show the dollar amount. Now, with the lower amount bill folded under the top bill; you give the money by putting your hand on the counter, palm down and drop the lower bill onto the counter quickly, putting your hand back in your pocket. It usually works with most people out in the suburbs; it works with this lady.

I grab the tickets, and walk over to Hec, slapping him lightly across the face a couple times to wake him up. "C'mon man, get up."

"What man?" he spits out with anger, his eyes still half way shut.

"The bus…It's takin' off soon."

"Man, I can't walk right now."

I grab his arm, swing it around my shoulder, and lift him up, pretty much dragging him across the floor. All kinds of people are staring at us as we walk by. I nod to each person with a half a smirk and quietly mouth that he tripped. Some ask if he's ok.

He just fell down the stairs…He ate a bad hot dog…A locker swung open and hit him in the face. Can you believe that?

I'm hoping no one notifies the police about a young man who is pretty much knocked out cold, or stops us to find out what's wrong: *What happened? Where are you going? What for?*

I just have to stay focused. I drag Hec down the hallway nervous as all hell. The overhead intercom notifies us that our bus is leaving very soon.

We walk outside, I notice our bus a couple lanes over and yell for the driver to get out and help me.

"My friend just tripped and fell over some luggage on the walk over here," I tell him as he throws Hector's other arm around his shoulder.

We get Hec into the bus.

"I'll take it from here," I say as the driver sits back in his seat.

I take Hec to the back of the bus, free of the inquisitive eyes I expect to see throughout the whole ride. I lay him down on one seat to let him sleep, then I take the seat right across from him. I watch some family members hugging and kissing each other goodbye. In the next bus over, I see all the people alone just sit down, cracking open their books. I hear a huge *swoosh* from the back as the brakes are released and we're on our way. But, before I decide to chill out for the entire ride, I slide over next to Hector, and start going through his pockets to see if he's got anything else worth taking. I find some tin foil. I fist it tightly and walk to the bathroom.

Inside the all-metallic chamber, I open the foil and find a few hits of acid. I decide to drop three, throw some water on my face, and return to my seat. I slide all the way to the end to get as close to the window as I can, looking out, but not really paying attention of what's out there. I guess, I'm to busy with all the thoughts in my head. You know going from one extreme to the next. Being a wanted man now, a convicted man. Hell, now I'll be a city man. I softly chuckle, liking the sound of that: The city man.

I'm gonna start all over, I tell myself. I'll get away for a while, get Anna off my mind...Geez, I miss her.

I look up at the ceiling of the bus and ask God, once again, to accept my apology for everyone I have hurt, and to let all of them know how sorry I am since I will no longer be around to do it. I ask God to help me out. To give me a sign, telling me I'm doing the right thing. For some weird reason I feel his presence around.

My spinal cord jiggles, sending the shakes from my neck to the top of my head. The first feeling of an acid trip. It's a sign, that I take for an answer to settle for the time being with only my thoughts and hallucinations. My journey is starting now.

I tell myself I will no longer put up with anyone's bullshit, not after this point forward. Even if I love them.

I love Hec, as a friend, and right now that's all that matters to me.

My head feels like pop from a two liter when you open it up for the first time. As if carbonation is down in the pit of my stomach, climbing its way up into my head until it fizzes, making it feel like my hair is moving from side to side without a breeze.

It's nighttime now. I'm still staring out the window. Half the people on the bus must be asleep. There are no lights on as we drive along the highway, and the lamplights are dimly lit. After a while, the individual light bulbs from the posts become one, transform into one beam of light as the highway dips up and down. I can't fall asleep. The LSD is kicking in harder than ever. Every time I shut my eyes, like a broken shade they roll right back up.

I look over at Hec. He's sound asleep, the acid makes him stretched out like one of those mirrors at the circus: elongated at one end and short and stubby at the other, under every passing light from the road.

I keep rubbing my head. I don't know why. It's addicting. It makes my head feel fuzzy all over and causes the stars to fall out of the sky and fly back up like a movie curtain.

I see Anna's clouded facial features; kind of like when it's cold out and you huff and fog up the window. It's like a mental picture framed as a masterpiece.

I think I see the outline of the big city nestled in front of the moon.

I think Hec is turning into a snake, slithering his body across all the bus seats.

The lamps above each head blink on and off.

The driver has a halo that glows and then evaporates away.

The bus deflates and expands.

I hear sirens. I see colorful clinking lights. I see my reflection in the window. I see myself as blue, red, white and black. I loom over to Hector's seat, but he's gone. Where did Hec go? Did he abandon me?

I start to get scared. I don't know where I'm going, don't know where I'm at. I don't know who to ask. I don't know anyone. I calmly get out of my seat and walk to the bathroom, trying not to look suspicious. I try to open the bathroom door, but it's locked. The lights from the highway start zooming by me faster and faster. White beams of light penetrate my eyeballs.

I can't see.

I keep trying to open the door. It won't open. I nudge it a little with my shoulder, turning the knob until it opens and I walk in looking over my shoulder. In front of me, I see the party from outside the front door, on the porch, and Anna is stepping inside the car. I run after her yelling, *"Wait!,"* but she doesn't hear me. *"Stop!"* She's looking in the other direction.

I'm banging on her passenger window. *"Open up!"* She still can't see me. The car engine starts. People are rushing out of the house. *"Wait!"*

There's a bottle in my hand. I look at it, wondering how it got there. Then, I see the lights from the cop car. I turn quickly, because I know what's coming. I see the cop running at me. I hold the bottle more tightly, waiting to swing. He gets closer and pulls out his club.

"Come on!" I yell at him.

Just when my arm is ready to strike, and his is ready to strike, I feel a hand grab my shoulder and turn me around. I strike him on the head, and then he grabs my head and bangs it against the bathroom wall.

I drop to the ground, finding myself in the bathroom.

Hec stands over me, huffing heavily with his clenched fists, ready to strike. I start to feel dizzy, and I lay down, crouching against the toilet. Hec moves my feet out of the way and sits down.

"Sleep well, brotha," he says softly. He then grabs the back of my head and slams it against the ground, knocking me out cold.

CHAPTER 15

❀

I wake up to the sound of a loud muffler and the smell of burning gas. My whole head is throbbing and pulsating from a bump on the back of my head, like a thumb jammed in a door. I wake up to the drool that has slid from my mouth into my nose. I had dreamt I was underwater. This is what woke me up. I thought the bus had fallen into a lake. I hop out of my seat, flapping my arms like I was doing the backstroke and looking around for the fastest way out. But no one else is leaving their seat. Hector is in the back with his head against the window, feet up on the seat, staring at me like I am a lunatic.

I drop my hands, after I notice everything is okay. It was all a dream. I wipe my lips from the drool dampening my flesh.

"My head hurts," I say loudly.

Rubbing the back of my head softly, I notice the old bump on the top of my head now has a twin brother, but I don't remember how the second one got there.

"Did I fall yesterday?" I ask with one eye open.

"You did more than fall, kid. You flipped out again," Hec replies with a half smile, shaking his head like my mother used to do when she was disappointed.

"Whaddya mean?"

"I had to put ya' to sleep, man, 'cause you were wiggin' out."

I want badly to know what happened, but when the sun's rays hit his left eye, seeing it all puffed up and yellow, I decide it would be better just to shut up. I put the back of my head against the cool window, hoping it will take down the swelling.

Hec and I just watch the landscape for the rest of the ride without speaking a word to each other. I don't think he is mad at me, or I at him. I am just scared about what might happen next when we get to the Big City. I think Hec is on the same wavelength, probably doubting everything about this trip and thinking about every "what if."

What if we run out of money?

What if his cousin won't let us stay with him?

What if the cops catch us?

What if there is a warrant out for me?

What if Hec and I have a falling-out?

What if…

What if…

Our first sighting of the city triggers a spooky feeling. Mobs of people living in a condensed area like ants inside their anthill, running mad all over the streets.

We watch the outline of skyscrapers standing as high as the sun, at least from a far distance. It gives me an adrenaline rush just knowing we're that much closer to a new world. I look over at Hec, who looks back at me and smiles. He nods his head up and down as if we are two guys hitting it big in Vegas.

We're almost there.

I ask Hec what his cousin is like, if he's cool, if he'll give us any problems if we ask to say for a while. Hec doesn't think so. He talks about him like he's been hanging out with him forever, but I honestly never heard him bring this kid up—never. He explains that he's a little different, and that's why he never talks about him. He didn't want the guys to know about him. I guess he thought we would make fun of him the way he is, but Hec won't explain or go into detail about what that "way" is. All he says is that he sells drugs, mostly weed, he thinks, and deejays at clubs whenever he can get a gig. His pad is a haven, a flophouse, sometimes filled with people who just come over and don't leave for weeks. Sometimes the place is empty. I guess he likes to share things, keep everything for the community, his community, his friends that come over and get kicked outta' the house, or friends of friends that don't have any other place to go.

I feel a little better, knowing it'll be okay for us to stay. After he has nothing else to say about his cousin, Hec just looks ahead at the city, which is getting bigger. As we get off the highway, he shakes his head. "Yeah, my cousin is just a little different, ya' know…He's just different."

We're walking down an old street. All the signs are in Spanish. No one around is speaking English. And the streets smell as if garbage had been stuffed into vents and someone with the special switch had popped them on to let the air blow and fill the city with this terrible smell.

"Yo chico, tu tienes dinero?"

"What did he say, Hec?"

"Don't worry about it. Just say no, and ignore him."

I smell hot Mexican food as we pass by an empty restaurant. It makes sense that I pick up something like that—I haven't eaten in a couple days, but my stomach hasn't growled until now.

"Hec, we need to get some food."

"After we get to my cousin's crib."

"How much longer?" I ask, wiping the sweat from my forehead.

"We're close."

Every street is filled with buildings. Each space is taken up like a prison cell, like the one I spent the night in after my rendezvous with the cops. I see people looking out their windows, looking into their windows as they hang out on their window sill to look outside at the next building across the street. Nothing but concrete walls and fenced-in properties. It reminded me of the billboard I read when I got off the bus. It said something like "once you come to the city, you'll never leave." It seems sorta true from looking around.

We keep walking down this street, going under a bridge. Subway cars pass above us, and below them a high brick wall holding up the whole structure that's covered with spray paint, covered with graffiti. The wall says something in old English, but it's just too cluttered to understand. Every car is honking at the car in front of it. People cross the street whether the light's red or green. Bums sit on the sidewalk, as I pass by, with all their possessions out in the open like they been living in that exact spot for weeks. They have grocery carts standing next to them filled with empty pop bottles. They have bags, tons of them tied to the cart. Most of them seem like they are completely surrounded by garbage. They have things all around them that they probably found in the dumpsters of alleyways that no longer holds value to someone, but worth something more to them, who have nothing.

Everyone I cross on the sidewalk wears backpacks. Are they off to school?

Young Mexicans are out at the corners, handing out pamphlets of pornography, laughing and talking to one another in Spanish. They bombard every passer-by with twenty different flyers of naked people, men and women. I throw my hand full of dirty pictures in the garbage.

This must be the city life? Non-stop noise in every direction, which is a lot different from the suburbs.

It's fast paced. You can see it in the way everyone walks. I try to keep up, but I'm way too tired and hungry for games. I want to sit down somewhere, anywhere to rest. I want to talk to Anna; I want to sleep in my bed, or any soft cushion that seems fit to rest my tired bones. There are so many things I want right now, but what I need is to stop thinking about the past.

As we continue to walk, I start to tell myself that this might have been a bad decision. But it's too late for regrets now. I know if I go back home, I'll definitely go to jail, so I have to cope. I have to be strong.

Hec starts to walk ahead of me. I think I'm starting to lag behind. I watch as he makes a right into a building. Before following him in, I stop and look up. Every window is open, most of them set behind steel bars and fire escapes, curtains are flapping all around from the wind, and potted plants sit on window sills. Hec is halfway up one flight of stairs when he stops and looks back at me, "Come on man, his place is up here."

I shrug and walk through the dark hallway, following him up the stairs. Most of the walls look cream colored, but I couldn't say for sure since most of it is covered in graffiti. I see men, as I pass the second floor, with no shirts on, standing by open apartment doors smoking as if they are waiting for something. I walk over little kids, playing on the stairwell to get to the next step. I say excuse me as I walk over them, but they don't acknowledge me, they don't even look up, as if I wasn't even there.

CHAPTER 16

❀

This is my fate, I tell myself. I'm sixteen years old and all I want are things to get better for me. I wish Anna could've made them better. I think about this as Hector's knocking on the door. When it opens, I'm surprised to see a woman open the door because I thought Hector said we were going to stay with his cousin, who I thought from the way Hector spoke about him, was a man.

"Mi primo Hector. Que Paso?" Says the woman in a manly tone.

"Nothin' man. What's goin' on?" Hector replies as he gives her a hug.

"Come in, come in," she says, "Who's your friend primo?"

"This is my boy Solomon. He lives by me."

I say hello and shake her hand. Her long finger nails feel fake, as they rub against my skin, they have a plastic feel about them.

"Hello! I'm Pablo most of the time, but right now you can call me Rita, ha,ha,ha!"

I smile, but deep inside I'm freaking out 'cause I've never met a real cross dresser before. Hell, I've never even met anyone who is gay. I'll have to talk to Hector about this later, I tell myself.

We walk over to the couch, which is right next to a huge window, giving a panoramic view of the city. As I look around, I notice that this apartment is pretty big, mostly made up of one huge open space.

The kitchen and living room are opposite of each other, but there's no wall or small ledge to separate the two. Where the living room starts and the kitchen ends there is a long hallway with a couple of closed doors on either side. The dining room table is in the middle of the big open space with a couple of people sitting around it, talking in Spanish. I see that they are weighing a mountain of weed, dividing it up into little baggies probably to sell on the street. They pay no attention to either of us. It is like we are invisible to them like the kids on the stairwell.

"Rita, you got anything to eat? We just took a long ass bus ride and haven't eaten in a couple days." Asks Hector with his head rested against the side of the couch.

"Mi casa es su casa," she says, taking a seat in a recliner that's opposite to the couch.

Hector gets up and walks to the kitchen, I get up and follow behind. I pass the table and look at the mountain of weed, wishing that was all mine.

Both of us start going through the cupboards. Hector finds a box of Twinkies.

"Are these ok to eat?" he yells from across the room.

"Yeah, I just went grocery shopping the other day."

Hec rips open the box and hands me a couple, taking a couple for himself and putting the ripped open box back in the cupboards. We walk back to the couch and take a seat, opening the packages with our teeth, spitting the plastic package into our palms, and putting the remains in between our thighs. We eat half of the Twinkies with one bite.

Rita swings back and forth in the recliner, pushing off each time with her high heels, staring at us eat, and taking a joint out of her curly black wig.

"So what brings you and your friend out here mi primo?"

"We're lookin' for a place to stay for awhile, and thought maybe you wouldn't mind," Hector replies with a mouthful of Twinkie.

"Oh...so you need a place to stay, huh? What's wrong wit your mother. Is she being difficult again?"

Hec nods his head as he rips open another package.

"...And what's your story, Chico, why you here?"

I swallow first and say, "Family problems too!"

"Huh." He stares at me, still rocking back and forth.

"Well, I guess I don't mind since you're family and all, Hector, but if you're gonna stay here you're gonna have ta help out," he says lighting up his joint.

"Like what?" Hector asks.

"Like helping me package the weed and other narcotics we distribute out onto the street. Right now, help is nil, honey, and I need two big strong boys to help me out, ha-ha-ha."

"That's cool with me cousin."

"How about you big boy, is that okay?"

"Sure," I say, shrugging my shoulders.

"Hec, you can sleep on the couch. Your friend, Solomon, right? You can sleep with me, ha-ha-ha."

My eyes get big and I look over at Hector, who's laughing with him.

"Haven't you ever crossed over, mama?"

"What the fuck are ya talking about?" I ask, feeling cross-examined, like when you play truth or dare, but with girls.

"Nothing hombre, just checkin.'"

Hec and I finish eating the Twinkies, then sit for a while as Rita gets up and walks to the table, picking up a handful of dope and dropping it into Hetcor's hands.

"How about you two smoke this, then I'll show you around. Sound good?"

"Yeah," Hec says as he stares at the pile of weed in his hand.

Rita walks away, winking at me.

We roll up a huge joint and smoke it, getting crazy high, and slouching down in the couch, smacking each other in the arm. I feel a little better now that I'm high and a little bit less uneasy about staying with a cross-dresser, having caught on that Pablo was just fucking around. It was hard to know at first with his sense of humor. I'm in a different crowd now, I tell myself. I gotta' fit in—in the big city.

Rita comes out of the hallway, but this time transformed and dressed as Pablo, wearing a blue mesh see-thru half-shirt and tight blue jeans. His hair is dark and short and very shiny. As he comes out, he starts to throw his hands all around in front of him, yelling in Spanish at the people sitting at the table.

"What's he saying?" I whisper to Hector.

"Oh, he's just tellin' them he'll be gone for awhile with family and if anything comes up short while he's away he kill 'em all and leave 'em in a garbage can."

We follow Pablo and his glittery silver purse out the door.

He takes us to the fashion district of the city. I walk behind the family, as they catch up in Spanish. Hec can speak it pretty well. I have no clue.

Pablo has one arm around him and his other hand resting on his hip, strutting like John Travolta.

The first place we go to is a thrift store. Pablo claims it has some of the hottest disco attire in the entire city. I don't know what the fuck that means, but I go along with it, figuring I have nothing to lose, since Hec and I came out here with nothing more than the shirts on our back. A couple of new threads can't hurt any. I don't want to smell on my first night out in the new town.

I find two pairs of jeans for $2 each and some regular shirts. Pablo goes against everything I pick out calling me normal and boring, then goes to the racks and pulls out some crazy bellbottoms and shirts with ruffles at the end of the sleeves. To make him happy I tell him it would look good on him, but I think of myself as a simple person. He shrugs, saying, "Fine, your choice, puto." But I run across a hat, just in case I see my face displayed anywhere. Hec doesn't grab anything, insisting that shopping is boring and that he just wants to hangout.

"Oh, poor baby, mommy still shopping for you?" Pablo exclaims, making me laugh.

Practically every store out here specializes in used clothing, which Pablo claims is one thing about the city we will have to get use to. Everyone has his own style, he says. Which, I believe, seeing other drag queens walking like hookers down the street, wearing fluffy scarves, crazy high heels, and airbrushed makeup. I even see men, in tightly fitted mesh shirts just like the one Pablo is wearing, with big brown blocky shoes. Pablo pays for everything, pulling out a pimp money roll at the register, proclaiming to the cashier that we were his kids and that his husband is out working hard. Hec and I just start laughing, going along with the gag, walking down the street and calling Pablo mom, and shit like that. Then, we stop at a diner, finally, to get some real food.

We sit down at the booth. The waitress brings our water and menus. Pablo knows her from some club and they start talking about music and the local club scene, and how it isn't the same since the yuppies from uptown started bombarding all the parties, getting into fights, and bringing in the cops, who shut down everything.

"It totally sucks ya know girl? You know what I'm sayin'? I won't even be able to take my children."

The waitress looks at us and smiles, like we are ten-years-old. When she walks away to check on another table, Pablo pulls out a vial and sticks his pinky finger with the long nail into it, pulling out white dust. He looks over his shoulder and inhales it into his nose. Then he offers me some, but I turn it down saying I only do that for special occasions.

"Well, you wouldn't call this a special occasion? I take you shoppin' and shit, give you a place to stay Chico…bhssss…Whatever, puto." He swings his hand in front of my face, waving it back and forth like he was brushing me off or something. But I give in and take a hit, and Hector does the same. Then we order some food and just hang out.

"Hector told me what happened to you mi hijo. Don't worry about nothin'. We'll keep you safe."

"Thanks," starting to feel fuzzy.

Pablo keeps talking, but I can't pay attention. The blast of the coke brushes over my body like a warm blanket. I look over Hector's shoulder, and see the background of the restaurant disconnecting like a TV screen out of service. I can hear them both on the other side of the booth laughing at me, pointing at me, but I can't pay attention. Slammed and stuffed, I light up a smoke just to stay calm.

"Your boy's fucked up, primo," I hear Pablo say to Hector, but in a real deep voice as if in slow motion.

"Yeah, he's fucking wasted," Hec says in an even deeper voice.

All I can do is sit still and laugh, feeling the hamburger I have just consumed turn all around my stomach, and the hairs on my arm as if they are standing straight.

Then I hear Anna calling me from behind my ear. Everything goes mute, except for the soft buzz of the telephone pole outside. I keep looking over my shoulder every few seconds to see if it would do it again, but it never comes back. Hec and Pablo get out of the booth, leaving me alone. Then, I think I see her, Anna, walking right past the doors to the kitchen as they flap back and forth. That's when Hector grabs my sleeve, yanking me out of the seat and pulling me forward till we're out in the street again.

Pablo comes up to me from behind and grabs my love handles, tickling me and making me laugh and squirm like I was covered with ants. That breaks me out of my shell and we walk down the street, messing with each other. The next stop is a coffee shop down a dark alley. On the side of one of the buildings is a half lit, blue neon light that says Caffeine in cursive with an arrow pointing down a stairwell.

Hector and I follow Pablo down and walk in. My first impression of the place is kinda scary, it reminds me of a low key joint that you need a special knock to enter. All the sockets in the ceiling are filled with red light bulbs. Round wood tables are scattered all across the single room coffee shop in no particular order with kids, maybe my age or a couple years older, hanging around, drinking outta white mugs with their back packs still attached. In the back is a stage that has two monster speakers that almost touch the ceiling with a pair of turntables resting in the middle.

Pablo finds an empty table. Hector and I follow, tiptoeing behind scrunched together chairs until we take a seat. A waitress walks up and asks us what we would like. Pablo answers by holding up three fingers, and saying three mugs.

The music playing sounds like aliens are about to land in the coffee shop, filled with tweaks and blurps behind a slow continuous strong beat. Pablo pulls his chair closer to the table and leans across saying, "This is where all the club kids hang out during the weekdays. It's a cool little spot for youngsters just wanting to chill out".

Hector and I nod our heads, digging the scene.

"I wish they had more places like this for us to hang out at," Hec suggests looking around.

The waitress walks back with three mugs in her hand and drops them on the table. Pablo gives her a couple dollars and tells her to keep the change.

"So, Sol what's up wit this girlie I hear Hec talk about?" Pablo asks, sipping from his mug.

"I don't know," I shrug. "Just some girl who got me into trouble that's all."

"I'm tellin' you hombre, you should stick wit your own kind; it's less of a hassle," Pablo declares winking at me.

"So, cuz you come here a lot?"

"All the time primo. This is where I make most of my dinero, ya know what I'm sayin'," Pablo says as he leans towards us.

"See half of these kids go to college around the corner, and most of em want to let loose for the weekends, or after a big test. So, I supply them wit what they need."

I continue to look around, seeing most of the kids packed in this joint are all wearing extra large blue jeans, sporting white visors on top of their head, and have sweatshirts three sizes too big. I guess they are part of this underground scene that most of the normal kids don't have a clue about. Pablo explains to us that there are these parties during the weekend, mostly in old abandoned warehouses. They usually begin at about ten at night and don't end till about six or seven in the morning. It's an all night dance party, playing nothing more than techno music. I guess a little faster than what's being heard now.

Pablo tells us he goes to these raves, I guess he calls them, every weekend, and pushes his product to all the kids who want to experience music on another level. He says the only problem with raves are they're illegal, and if cops show up, everyone will get a ticket for disturbing the peace, and if you get caught with anything on you, you could be screwed for a long time.

"I don't think I'll be going to those," I yell over the loud music.

"You might have to eventually, if you're gonna start working for me," Pablo announces with a smile.

The rest of the evening we just sit around, listening to music, and drinking mounds of coffee. I don't think I've ever drank so much in my life. I'm wide awake, being close to feeling like I am on a hit of acid. The down side, I learn after riding home in the cab is that after every couple of minutes, I have to tell the cab driver to pull to the side so I can run out and take a piss on the side of the street. Over all, it still is a good first night in the city.

CHAPTER 17

❈

"Hello," I hear her say in a sweet angelic voice.

"Hey, Anna, it's Sol."

"Where are you? Everyone's looking for you!" She says with urgency, like she was expecting me to call. "Everyone at school has been asking about you, even taking me out of class to see if I know anything."

"Really? Are you okay? I didn't get you in trouble, did I?"

"No, but the cops came over one night, and asked me a lot of questions."

"I'm sorry," I whisper into the pay phone, hoping the bum right next to me doesn't catch me getting mushy.

"You're in a lot of trouble, Sol."

"I know."

"What are you gonna do?"

"I don't know. Do ya miss me? Are ya still seeing that moron?"

"I don't wanna get into that. What are you gonna do?"

"Do you miss me?"

"What are you gonna do, Sol?"

"Just answer the question?" I insist, but I hear only silence.

"Sol, it's not ea…VROOM."

"What I can't hear you"

"VROOM"

I hang up the phone, acting like I got disconnected, not wanting to hear her answer because the way she started to say it, I knew it was gonna be bad.

I'm sorry Anna.

I walk back across the street to Pablo's apartment, where Hec is sitting at the dining room table, weighing weed and sticking it into plastic Baggies. I sit at the table next to him and start helping out. Pablo says he'll pay us fifty dollars for every pound we weigh and push off. Right now, both of us are at four pounds. We're high and we're pinching a little and putting it into our pockets. We're planning to get our own place, just Hec and me.

Later, we're going to some party, a friend of Pablo's, an artist. A "good connection," as Pablo puts it.

I guess, he's been selling shit for a while now, and does gigs as a DJ whenever the opportunity presents itself. Hec tells me that this is the main reason Pablo moved out here in the first place: to become a DJ. It is also a little more acceptable to be gay and different in the city than, say, where we live.

I guess he got into the biz, when an ex-boyfriend of his, who was dealing drugs at the time, got shot to death. Pablo took over his business and territory.

"He was like the first homosexual drug dealer in the city, he even whooped some ass when he had to, to show kids that he wasn't some lush faggot, and that he could handle his own."

His operation is pretty simple. He gets some right over the Mexican border, weighs and packages the dope, then gives it to street kids to sell. I guess, he asks for all the money up front, when giving it to the street kids, who in turn triple their money when they sell it on the street. So, Pablo could be making triple of what he's making now, but he doesn't want to get greedy, because most of those street kids usually get busted or shot in the street.

"My cousin's a business man, not some peddler!" says Hector.

Hec tells me that Pablo's really happy that we came out here, since now he won't have to pay those Mexicans anymore. I guess they were ripping him off.

Instead of walking the distance to the party, the three of us are supposed to take a cab, my first time in one.

Pablo is Rita tonight, rockin' a bright purple, shoulder length wig that bops and curls at the end, and on top of her hair are big bug-eyed sunglasses. Rita's skirt is made of shiny silver that drops below her thighs with a matching handbag on her forearm. The purse is filled with a vial of coke for the night, cigarettes in a leopard print case, twelve ribbed condoms, and a pimp-roll the size of my fist.

Before we walk out the door, Rita steps out of her room singing "*I got two guys on my side*" with a Latin accent. One look at us slouching on the couch, finishing a white line and some herb smoke, and she yells out, "No, no, no! I ain't goin' out with two guys looking like that. You mus' be crazy!"

We have on what every young man would wear on any given day—blue jeans, shirts, and gym shoes. We start to laugh as Rita gets all pissed off because we look like shit and I guess she wants to show us off.

She runs back into her room and comes back out with an armful of clothes, which she drops on the ground. She points to the pile and says, "Choose!"

Hec and I get off the couch and crawl to the pile. I swim in it and laugh hard with Hec. We start wrestling around, wrinkling all the clothes. Rita yells out that we need to chill out and get ready.

"Look what you two putas are doing to my clothes. Stop that! Stop that!"

I grab Rita by the legs while lying on the ground, feeling like I'm floating without gravity and start yanking and telling her to love me. Hec grabs the other leg and starts yelling the same thing. "Beat me Rita…beat me. We're your slaves."

"Get off me. Get the fuck off me," she keeps yelling, her arms flailing to avoid a fall. Catching us off guard, she whips off her purple wig and says, "Fuck it!" in a masculine voice and jumps on top of both of us and starts banging the shit out of us. Pablo holds us down and gives us Charlie horses all across our thighs. Then, he starts going for our nuts, grabbing our crotches and yelling that he is gonna amputate.

After beating the shit out of us, he gets off the floor.

For a gay, Pablo's strength surprises me. He snorts a big ol' line from the coffee table and says, "You two women get up and get dressed. You're my dates tonight," in the voice of the fabulous Rita Martinez. "And if you don't put on something else than those dirt clothes, I'll kick your ass."

I walk out of the apartment and into the cab wearing baggy, gray pin-stripped pants with a bright yellow-ribbed shirt, which I didn't like, because I was getting so skinny you could see my ribs. I put on a furry red Kango hat. Hec sports bright blue parachute pants with a fake mink coat, and another pair of Rita's sunglasses.

That's how we leave to the artist's party.

Rita tells us we look so disco, so chic. I say we look like Huggy Bear from Starsky and Hutch. Hec thinks we look like mentally retarded Mexicans, to which Rita replies with a *fuck you* and pulls out a cigarette holder from her purse, lights a smoke, and bangs on the back of the cab's seat, yelling at the driver to go faster. "We're gonna miss the party, estupido."

CHAPTER 18

❀

I feel as if I'm a tiny tumbleweed drifting through the crowds of people who I see as a field of wild flowers inside an old warehouse. Every skin color that God created is at this party. Black people with Jimi Hendrix hair-do's and bell bottoms. White kids, some who look like those kids we saw a couple days ago at the coffee shop, sporting big pants that cover their shoes. Other white kids all around who have afro wigs and big round sunglasses. I see those Gothic kids that are draped in the color black. I see a couple Indian kids with turbans on their head smoking out of a bong. I see Chinese and Japanese, men dressed as women, women dressed as men. All the colors of skin that God created are here that resembles a field filled with every flower imaginable, in every color.

I look up to these beautiful people who remind me of flowers and categorize them as bright petals, red roses, and white daffodils as they illuminate and glow like paintings I've seen of the Garden of Eden. My mind begins to wander farther off, as I think of these people being hand picked by God himself, placed here, at this warehouse, as a marvel of his excellence at creation.

I wander off to the refreshment table that has bowls filled with colorful candy: red, orange, yellow, and blue. A punch bowl is filled to the rim with a light green substance that fizzles and steams at the top. I stand by the table wasted, not knowing what to grab first. A man walks towards me with long curly brown hair, and a thick beard, who is cloaked in a white sheet.

"Who are you suppose to be?" I ask in a long drawl.

"I'm Jesus my son, and I would have to say you look somewhat puzzled?"

"I don't know what to eat first?"

"Try a little of everything, it's fruit picked from paradise," he speaks as if he is a LP record played on 45.

"Always remember if you miss your mother, take a large dose of H, it'll feel like she's hugging you no matter where you are."

"But what if I don't take H?" I ask, seeing him in three different places.

"Then, take Demerol, it's not as comforting as your mother hugging you, but it's like that blanket you love to cuddle into when it's cold…Here try some."

He puts a bunch of pills in my mouth, sticks both hands into the punch bowl and lowers my head into his hands to drink.

I swallow the pills.

He places his hands on both sides of my face and kisses my forehead, then backs up a few steps saying, "God loves you." Then, walks away.

I look out the window in front of me into the night sky and see countless stars hiding behind skyscrapers, apartment buildings, and bridges. They are hiding out as if their light doesn't feel bright, and they don't want to be seen by others.

One in particular sort of shows itself halfway behind a building in front of me.

I close my right eye for a second and it disappears. When I open my eye, it shows only half of itself, playing a game of hide-and-seek.

I did another line after that, and thought about how cool if someone was actually sitting on that star playing that game with me.

I close my eye again and open it back up. I keep playing until both of my eyes close. I don't feel like opening them back up. It's too much of an effort like when you drift in and out of consciousness while sitting in bed watching TV. Then, I feel myself being lifted off the ground, and I tell myself that leaves, petals, hands, Jesus—whatever are picking me up and carrying me off to heaven. They carry me until I feel a chill, which tells me I'm back out on the street.

After a couple moments, I feel warm again, and I see Rita combing my hair with her fingernails, telling me everything is gonna be all right. "We're almost home."

"I saw Jesus tonight", I say before passing out. "He fed me Demerol."

"I know honey…I see Jesus every night. He's one of my biggest clients."

I close my eyes in satisfaction, as if my favorite blanket when I was child, the light blue one with a picture of a little boy sitting on a star with the blue satin lining, is wrapped around me. I close my eyes again with a comforting smile. The city lights and sounds were my musical mobile like the ones baby's have that hang above their crib to fall asleep. I am at peace for the first time since that night at the party; I hope tomorrow I will be re-born.

I awoke on a couch. Pablo's couch.

I've been holding it in for what feels like hours until I can't hold it any longer. My bladder is gonna pop. I get up, feeling like my head is a brick, and stumble along the hallway until I reach the bathroom. I switch on the light, squint my eyes, and take a leak that seems to last forever.

Suddenly, I notice myself in the mirror.

I tell myself that my name is Solomon.

I tell myself that I am Solomon, who is moving up in the world.

I tell myself that I am Solomon who once had a beautiful girlfriend.

I am only Solomon who likes to do drugs. I think I need help, but I won't admit it to others.

I'm home alone, sleeping on the couch until I am awoken by what sounds like a trumpet note that will not end. Looking out the window, I see a black SUV with tinted windows, blaring its horn while flashing it's brights at a bum standing in the middle of the street.

It oddly resembles a matador and bull: a face-off, old-school style. The bum just stands there yelling back at the truck. "Fuck…off…suck my dick!" You can tell whoever is inside is getting a little pissed off, because he revs the engine after each obscenity. I hide myself, getting a strange premonition that something bad is about to go down.

The bum starts yelling louder, asking the driver to hook him up. "C'mon man…I'll give ya the money…hook a brotha' up."

But the SUV remains still. Nobody comes out of the truck to tell this bum to fuck off. The bum picks up a bottle off the street and throws it at the car. When it lands on the windshield, I know it's bad news. I see the back taillights turn on for a second. The wheels squeal, causing smoke at the back end, and moves forward.

But the bum doesn't budge.

As the SUV comes at him full force down the empty street, I want to yell out to the dumb prick to move, but I get scared. I freeze, telling myself the truck won't hit him, it won't hit him.

But the SUV hits the bum on the left side, causing him to fall underneath the truck and get run over with the front and back tires. It's the first time I have ever seen someone get hit and run over by a car.

I hear a beeping sound. The truck is going into reverse, stopping just as the back bumper is kissing the bum's head. The driver's door opens and a big black guy gets out. He is wearing a black suit and dark shades, and a big necklace dangles from his neck. This should be important for the person who calls the cops to give a description. Any minute I should be hearing sirens.

He walks over to the bum, shaking his head.

"Fuck you, punk," he yells at the dead guy, or at least that's what I think he says. I watch as he kicks him a couple times in the stomach with his foot.

Adjusting his sports coat, he looks up in my direction. I lean quickly away from the window, keeping one eye on the street. He smiles as he looks up and gets back in the SUV and drives off, leaving the dead bum in the street. I don't hear any sirens, or anyone screaming for help. Everybody who walks by just leaves him there, to die.

I can't go back to sleep after seeing that. I just sit on the couch in the dark playing over the hit-and-run in my head, again and again.

The next day, I tell Pablo about it, but he sort of snickers.

"Fuckin' Sly," he says, smoking a cigarette.

"That boy never fucks around."

"Who's Sly?"

"He's a pusher, a bad ass on the other side of town. He usually comes out this way to go to the nightclubs. I bet some bum asked to cop some shit for free and Sly told him to fuck off. The boy's bad. He don't fuck around." And he leaves it at that, going back to rolling up the dope and cutting the crack.

I light a smoke, feeling quite unsettled. But I hide it, going back to work, trying not to ask any more questions. I don't understand why the man had to die. That's what scares me, death. I'm having second thoughts about staying out this way after seeing that, almost hopped on a train last night back home to turn myself in, but I didn't. The best remedy, I think, is to get high. That will take my mind off this.

CHAPTER 19

❀

Tonight Hector and I have our first job as dealers, which is about time since it's starting to get really lame sitting at the kitchen table all day measuring shit and putting into little Baggies.

Pablo informs us that he wants us to go to his friend Trina's loft tonight because she's throwing a party, an acid party. He says we should have no problem making money since we will be the only ones supplying the party with LSD.

"She's real cool amigos ok, so don't give her any *sheeit* comprehende?"

We both nod our heads.

"What's she do?" I ask, hoping she might be cute.

"Girlfriend's a hair-dresser for a drag club downtown."

"OH!" Hector and I exclaim in frustration, having to spend our night hanging out with men dressed as women, tripping on acid with no real women to hit on.

"Can't we do somethin else? Shit like that really isn't our scene," Hector states as he walks over to the kitchen table to light a joint.

"Yo puto, I don't give a god damn what your scene is, if you want to make a little extra dough, you gots to do this for me cause I have other plans tonight," Pablo insists snapping his fingers all around Hector's face, looking like a stuck up sorority chick.

"We'll do it!" I exclaim figuring anything is better right now than sitting around all night.

Pablo walks to his bedroom and comes out with a Ziploc bag filled with what looks like index paper.

"These are the sheets of acid," he says handing the baggie to me.

As I look over at the sheet, I notice small little pictures of yellow sunshines all across each sheet. A hundred little yellow sunshines to be exact, meaning a hundred hits of acid were in each sheet, giving us a total of four sheets, which makes four hundred hits of acid at 5 dollars a piece. Meaning we should pocket somewhere around two thousand dollars, give or take a few c-notes cause I know I'll have to eat at least four to cope with the insanity of being at a drag party.

With the bag in my hand, I look over at Hector, who's looking back at me with a big smile, which pretty much means with this much stuff in our possession, we might have to take it back to our style of selling.

Back in the day, when Jug gave us a bag full of weed to sell to the kids at school, both of us would first pinch a few big buds outta the bag. Then, sell it to the kids at a few dollars extra, putting the extra money directly in our pockets. In the end, we would be able to get high, give the profit to Jug, and have a little money for ourselves, which we spent at Pizza Hut and the movies every night for as long as it lasted.

"This is your first opportunity to show me what you can do, and if you putos pull this off that means I'll have more in store for you two in the future, like sex changes or some shit like that," Pablo mumbles, laughing as he walks back into his bedroom.

I stick the bag in my pocket, grab a couple of joints, and run to Hector, who's sitting on the couch. I jump on top of him and put him in a headlock, taking my fist and rubbing it into his hair, "You like that punk, huh? You like that?"

"Get off me woman," he yells grabbing the back of my neck and pulling me back.

We wrestle around for a moment like we use to at home when someone gave us something to do besides sit around. I remember when Hector use to spend the night in my room, in the morning who ever was the first one up would have to jump on top of the other and sorta lightly hit him to scare the shit outta him. We haven't done something like that in a while.

Hopefully after tonight, Hec and I can start a little fund for us to save for a place of our own. So I can beat him up in the morning in our own place, not having to worry about waking up Miss Sleeping Beauty who needs her twelve hours of sleep daily.

We get to the loft quickly, taking a cab, instead of the subway. We wanted to take the subway since neither of us has ever been on one before. But, Pablo went against it, saying we might get lost and tonight isn't a good time to get lost with a pocket full of acid and dope.

Hector knocks at the door.

"So how much should we sell these hits for," I ask Hector, staring at the peephole in the door, which exposes a small ray of light from inside. I'm waiting for the hole to become dark, meaning that someone's black pupil is looking at us from the other end, and the door should open.

"I don't know Sol. Do you think we should do something like this to my cousin and his friends?"

"Why the hell not," I exclaim. "We did it to our own friends in the past. What makes your cousin so special?"

"Well, he did give us a place to stay, ya know, and he's letting us help him with the business."

"Fuck off," I whisper into his ear still watching the peephole illuminated with light.

"If we're gonna become big hens in the coup, ya know we're gonna have to crack a few eggs, right?" I tell him.

"I guess. So, then how much do we sell them for?"

"I don't know. What do you think?"

Hector looks at me with a look of annoyance. "Why are you asking me jerk off, this your idea. You should have it all planned out if your gonna pull it off stupid."

"Ok.Ok," I holler back. "How about eight dollars a hit. What's taking them so long to open the door?"

I knock on it again.

"Eight dollars!" Hector shouts. "Eight dollars. Who in their right mind is gonna buy a hit of acid for eight dollars when the going rate is five. Don't you think it should be a little lower? I was like thinking seven?"

I continue to stare at the peephole, doing the math in my head to see if seven dollars a hit will make us any extra cash.

"Ok.Ok," Hector states. "How about seven fifty?"

"Seven fifty? Whadda we sellin' hotdogs? What if they ain't got the fifty cents, are we gonna wait as they shift through their pockets for change. Or wait, I got an idea, how about I run to the bank real quick and get some quarter rolls, so when they give us eight dollars, I'll at least be able to give them change," I say shaking my head at his stupid remark.

Hector stands quietly for a moment. I hope registering everything he just told me. "Yeah, seven's good."

"Thank you."

The peep hole finally becomes black and we both hear the sounds of locks clanging back and forth until the door opens up just a nudge with a head popping out. A girl's head with multi-colored hair.

"Yeah?" She asks looking at both of us like we're weirdoes.

"We're here for Pablo," I declare, trying to look tough.

"Oh, ok. Why don't you two come in?"

A strong breeze passes through both of us as the door opens up, turning this quiet hallway into an enclosed Mardi Gras. The bass from the music pounds on the walls, making it tremble and echo through our ears as we walk through the hallway of the loft. The girl walks behind us and closes the door, and then jumps back in front of us with a big smile, looking like a deranged lunatic with her multi-colored hair.

"Hi," she yells. "I'm Trina."

We both shake her hand as we introduce ourselves.

"Come on," she says. "Follow me to the party."

As we pass through her hallway, seeing framed pictures across the walls of women with different colored hair, posing for head shots, I notice that some of these men dressed up as women don't look too bad.

"Did you do all their hair?" I ask trying to make conversation.

"Yup," she hollers. "It's my art."

As we enter her living room we see a bunch of people with big colored wigs on, dancing around—afros in yellow, bee hives in pink, shoulder length hair in purple, even shaved heads bleached yellow with black circles dyed on top.

In the middle of the living room dance floor, hanging from the ceiling is a big disco ball twirling around. There is a DJ in the back of the room, with a huge black afro, pulling out records and putting em on the turntables, bopping his head up and down. On one of the walls is a movie screen, showing people laughing with their wigs on, making faces into the camera, kissing, hugging, and just having a good time.

"Yeah, that screen is showing everyone at the party right now. It's hooked up to a camcorder that's being passed," Trina hollers grabbing my arm and showing me around.

I see Hector walking behind us, just staring around the room like a lost child in a department store. He looks a little uneasy as we pass through the mobs of people dancing all around. Some wink at him, others run up and give him a hug. To us these people look crazy, but I bet to them, seeing us just in T-shirts and jeans, we look equally weird.

Strobe lights are flashing all around the room. Trina with her arm in mine walks me over to the corner of the room, where a group of people are just standing around, drinking, talking, and laughing.

This reminds me of a school dance, with a 70's disco theme.

Hector and I stand to the side as Trina talks to the group of people. We can't hear what they're saying because the music's so loud, but we know she's talking about us since we see Saturday Night Fever and the gang look back at us every few seconds. Trina comes outta the group and grabs my arm again and says, "follow me."

We walk over to the DJ booth, and she stops us to the side, as she walks over to the afro bopping music man and says something in his ear. I watch as he continues to bop his head up and down. Then, he turns his attention to his turntables, taking two switches on the mixer and bringing them down, making the music slowly disintegrate.

Trina walks over behind the DJ and grabs a microphone, plugging it into the back of the mixer. I look over at Hector, who looks back and shrugs. We both have no idea what's going on.

Everyone stops dancing, and looks over at the DJ with Trina standing to his side ready to speak in the microphone. As the people just stand around in their funny hair-do's, and huge sunglasses, and crazy clothing: tight metallic shirts, big fluffy scarves, and platform shoes. I notice there have to at least be almost a hundred people at this party, and being crazy loud, I'm surprised the cops haven't showed up yet. This makes me nervous.

The parties I usually go to back home don't have as many kids as they do here, and the music's not as loud, but the cops seem to come and break it up without fail.

Trina's neighbors share a wall with her. They have to hear what the fuck is going on, they have to be pissed unless squares don't live in the city?

"Hi everyone," Trina hollers in a high pitched voice. "I would like to thank everyone for coming tonight, and I hope you all have a great time. The reason I stopped the music was for the two special people who just showed up."

Hector and I look at each other, hoping she isn't talking about us, but we know she is. She continues, "These guys are friends of Pablo's. You guys know Pablo, our favorite Mexican? Anyways, they've come to bring this party to another level. They've come to expand our minds, so if any of you would like to get a little crazy just ask them to do it for you!"

Everyone begins to cheer, yell, and clap their hands. A big white light suddenly appears on Hector and me, blinding us as we put our hands in front of our face, and squint. I watch Hector wave.

"LET'S GET CRAZY!" Trina yells as the music builds back up.

The music builds back up and everyone goes nuts dancing around and jumping up and down screaming. Hector and I decide to set up operations in the bathroom.

On our way can see the red in everyone's eyes, the hunger for LSD. You can tell everyone wants some, and I don't care if you are gay or dress like a woman, if you want it bad enough, you'll do anything to get it.

The bathroom is small with bright yellow tiles, and covered in this shag pink carpet from the bath mats to the toilet cover. Hec walks right into the bathtub, pulling the curtain all the way to the other end, and laying down, resting his melon right on top of the faucet. If he's deciding to hide from everyone, then it would be smart to give him the acid, keeping only a couple hits on hand for the patrons. I sit down on the side of the tub, pulling down the toilet cover, and ripping off the shag carpet to use as a desk, or an operating table. I make sure the door is still closed, making it look on the other side that we're not open for business yet. Before settling in and making that money, I knock on the inside of the door for a second, hoping someone's standing right next to it, and opens it up. A small little guy, like myself, with a baldhead, opens the door just an inch to look inside.

"Did ya knock, dude?" He asks.

"Hey bud, if you bring a bottle of some strong alcohol and some orange juice for my friend, I'll give you a hit of acid for free," I say holding up a piece of sunshine in between my fingers.

"You got it," he utters as he shuts the door.

I turn to my side for a second, pulling on the shower curtain to take a look at Hector, who at about this minute, has that crazy look in his eye with a huge smile on his face watching the tiled ceiling. I stick the bag in his pants, smack his face a couple times, and kiss his forehead, feeling like a million bucks cause that's what I'm hoping to make tonight. The baldheaded guy knocks first before coming in and has everything I ask for in his hand. He puts it on top of the toilet and steps back. I grab the carton of orange juice and stick it behind the curtain, laying it on Hector's chest. Then, I place the quart of Jim Beam next to my feet. I take a hit of the sunshine acid and a put it in his hand. He immediately sticks it on his tongue.

"See the guy sitting in the tub?" I say pointing my thumb behind my shoulder.

The baldheaded guy nods.

"Good, he's my right hand man, so if anyone gives us any trouble, he'll pop outta there and start trouble, and nobody here wants trouble with a mean Mexican like that. Catch my drift?"

He nods again.

"Good. Is there a line out there?" I ask.

"Yeah. A long one," he says.

"Ok. You can leave now."

He nods his head one last time, almost as if he was bowing and opens the door, walking out. I sit for a second grabbing two hits and sticking them in my mouth, then I walk over to the door and open it, yelling at the top of my lungs, "Open for business!" over the loud house music that's bumping in the back.

I sit back down on the toilet and watch as mobs of drag queens in big beehive wigs, and short patent leather mini skirts walk in with money in their hand ready to buy some acid. All I do is take the money, swig on the bottle, and begin to hallucinate.

In an hour most of the sunshine acid is sold, except for a couple hits I decide to hold onto for Hec and myself. The bottle of Jim Beam is half way gone, and my ass is about numb from sitting on the white porcelain tub for such a long time. I get up and walk outta the bathroom, knowing I can leave Hector alone since he's off somewhere else, still lying in the bath tub.

The music is still pumping hard, and I notice pretty much everyone is wasted on the dance floor, shaking their ass. I lean against the wall, feeling a huge head rush, and feeling the acid kick in like a bag of rocks dropped on my head. First, the trails set in, which are wavy lines in my vision, making everything look as if it is under water. Right now, everyone reminds me of that cartoon I watched as a child called the Snorkels, in which, these little sea creatures ran around and danced at the bottom of the sea.

Also, the color of everything gets heightened, like those big pink wigs bopping up and down on the dance floor. Not only are they pink on acid, but fluorescent pink. Black people become invisible where there is no light. White people become translucent when standing in direct light.

The song playing over the speakers makes my head bob a little. It has this lady in a chipmunk voice yelling over and over again—*red light, green light*. When red light is heard the music stops, and everyone stops dancing, then when they hear green light the music kicks back in, and everyone begins dancing again like the drug dance version of Simone Says.

A black man or woman, I can't tell the difference at this point, grabs my arm and yanks me on the dance floor. I stand in place, watching this person shake their hips from side to side, and wave their arms in all directions. I feel someone behind me, rubbing their ass against mine. A woman is freaking me, grabbing my ass. Two people from my side grab both of my arms and start to wave them from side to side. Big faces with big grins are right in my face, laughing out loud, and moving in all directions. I see my feet moving, but I wouldn't call it dancing. I guess everyone else does as they continue to pass me from one person to the next shaking their asses in front of my crotch, grabbing my ass, and rubbing my chest as the beat leads them into these movements—*Red Light…Green Light…*

The next day, I wake up in the bath tub, lying right next to Hec. The curtain is closed and I'm not ready to open it just yet. I jump on top of Hector, who is still sleeping, and smack him very lightly in the face until he gets the point and opens his eyes. Then, all of a sudden they become huge like grapefruits, and Hec begins to scream at the top of his lungs like a little girl, wiggling back and forth trying to get outta the tub.

"What the fuck are you doing?" I yell moving over to the side to let him up.

Hec jumps outta the tub, and stands on the pink shag floor mat, rubbing his eyes, and looking back at me, almost like he doesn't recognize me. Then, he starts laughing.

"What's so funny?" I ask still lying in the tub. He doesn't say a word just holds his stomach and continues laughing. "Waddya laughing at dip shit?"

"Have you looked in the mirror, Sol?" He asks looking for a hand held mirror in the bathroom.

"Why?" I ask getting a little freaked out.

"Wait a minute jerk off, I'll show you," Hec says shuffling through the drawers.

He pulls out one of those small mirrors that has a handle, and hands it to me with the mirror part looking the other way. As I turn it around I notice my shaved head is no longer black, but bleached yellow, bright yellow.

"Holy shit," I holler feeling my dry scalp. "I look like a frat boy!"

Hector continues to laugh. "Now you look like one of them," he hollers.

"Who the fuck did this to my head?"

"What did you do last night?" Hector asks touching it for himself.

"I don't remember," I utter still half asleep.

As we both got outta the bathroom, and back out into the loft, we both notice people lying all over the place, on the floor, on the couch, on the kitchen table wrapped in blankets, on chairs wrapped with another body on top of them. Then, out walks Trina in a leopard print robe, who just walks right up to me, grabs the back of my head, and sticks her tongue in my mouth. When she finishes, she looks at me with piercing eyes and says, "I dyed it to remind me of the sunshine acid, you became my piece of art."

She walks away, down the hallway into a room, closing the door behind her.

Hector looks at me again, asking, "What did you two do last night?"

"I don't fucking know," I whisper as we walk to the door.

We take a cab back to Pablo's apartment; I tell Hec as we get outta the car that I'll be right up.

"Ok blondie," he says laughing up the stairs.

I walk across the street to the pay phone right out front from the fruit market.

As I grab the phone about to make a call, I see a head pop outta the window, yelling, "YEAH BABY! YOU LOOK HOT! I KNEW YOU WERE GAY."

It's Pablo, shaking his hands up in the air like a Vegas dancer, laughing out loud, with Hector standing behind him, laughing like crazy. I give them both the middle finger and make my phone call.

CHAPTER 20

❀

She says it was her fault. She's sorry. She wants me to come back home.

That's what Anna says, as I look over to the Mercado with its fresh display of fruits.

"If I didn't pull that stunt with Calvin, none of this would've happened," Anna exclaims tearfully and sniffs on the other end.

"It's okay, honey," I say, trying to sympathize. "Things just happen. I'm not mad, honest."

I'm lying. I was quite furious, and I get more pissed off when she spits the name Calvin from her mouth. When I got here it didn't hurt so bad. It was almost like a memory of something that happened long ago; something I recalled only bits and pieces of.

Anna warns me that I'm burying my feelings deep inside myself, so they won't show, but that this made it much easier for me to leave on a whim.

I don't buy it, though—her counseling. It's all just a trap. For all I know the cops are on the other line listening in, tracking my exact location right now.

For all I know in a few seconds, while I have the perfect size orange in my sights, the cops could pop out of nowhere, circling the payphone with squad cars, ordering me to stay still.

I think how I would slowly hang up the phone while Anna's crying like mad. But before I hang up, I put the phone piece to the side of my face and calmly whisper to her, "You make me want to die," and hang up, staring the cops in the eye.

They have their pistols trained on me, cocked back and ready to put a couple of slugs into my chest if I should make the wrong move.

And what is my next move?

I know it isn't pretty. I take a cigarette out, light it up with a pack of matches, and take a couple puffs. Then, I fling it to the ground and in slow motion yell so loud that I feel my veins pop out of my neck. I feel every bone and muscle in my body tighten up. My yelling starts to shatter windows, it turns the sky black, and the cops have no choice but to start shooting, blazing up the phone booth with copper bullets. And I die, with a smile on my face as the hail of bullets simmer and the sky returns to a blue hue.

"Solomon…Solomon…Hello."

I must have drifted off.

"Yeah, I'm still here."

"I was thinking, if you come back home, you can get that help, maybe tell the cops you got scared and ran. Let them know you have a problem. They'll help you," Anna says excitedly.

"I don't know Anna. I don't think I can do it. I love you and without you being there I don't know if I can make it alone. At least over here I got Hec, someone around I can trust. I'm sick of playing Mr. Tough Guy. I just want all this to go away. I mean, I wish it would all just disappear."

"I know…I know."

I change the subject, feeling my high come down. I'm ready to inject more junk into my brain to continue this conversation, but I don't have any on me right now. I feel my hands start to tremble. I feel sweat on my forehead.

She tells me school's out. She graduated. She'll be leaving for college at the end of the summer. But, she says if she doesn't see me soon she'll come out here looking for me before college classes begin.

The only thing I can think of saying is, "You promise?" But, before I do, I hang up, staring at the black SUV with the tinted windows double-parked in front of Pablo's building with its hazards blinking.

CHAPTER 21

❀

Drug dealers only use pay phones.

Drug dealers never have a regular phone in their homes.

They possess a power of speech, able to turn water into wine, so to speak.

Most dealers are known to be paranoid.

Few are rarely without a piece.

This is what Pablo talks about when he and I are alone. This is my education.

If they're hooked, they'll have mad supplies of tissues in their pockets from snot constantly running down their nose.

A real drug dealer trusts no one.

A real dealer has no heart.

It's a cutthroat business.

A corporation.

An enterprise.

Today, there is a meeting between Pablo and his affiliate from the other side of town—Sly, the scary guy driving the black SUV that smothered a bum into road kill. I guess there's a territory open out in the suburbs. The controller of that district took a nasty spill.

He's dead.

It's open territory for whoever wants to run it. That's what Sly and Pablo need to discuss. But I've also heard that most situations like this are bad news. This is when a dealer who wants to discuss the opportunity with an associate winds up getting greedy and killing the other, which ends the meeting, and simplifies the decision of who gets what in the open district.

I'm working at the table, rolling up bags, weighing the grass, cleaning mirrors. Sly's on the couch, his legs spread out, open big like the letter V. Pablo's sitting on the other side of the room, his legs crossed and holding a coffee mug against his lips, a sign of nervousness.

Hector is in the bedroom sleeping.

"All right, kid, this is how we gonna do thangs for now on, ya hear," Sly embarks in street slang. "That punk ass bitch is outta the picture, ya know. How do ya wanna divide the open market?"

Pablo turns his head to the window, looks out, and ponders his answer. You can tell he knows that saying the wrong thing would be a problem, especially since Sly's last kill was just the other night. That thought must have illuminated Pablo's mind when he asked the next question.

"Well, I have a couple ideas, hombre. But, I'd like to hear what you have to say first." Pablo says as he looks over at me, constantly moving his eyes over to the right.

As I follow the path he leads with his eyes, I make the connection that he wants me to leave, which upsets me because I really want to see what this guy Sly is all about.

I walk out of the living room and go into the bathroom shutting the door behind me. I can hear them mumbling through the paper-thin walls but make out only bits and pieces of their conversation. How I want to hear what two drug dealers talk about.

But this is pretty much my first chance to get fucked up alone without anyone being around. I pull out a couple of rocks from my pocket that I took off the table. Then, I cut them up and snort it up my nose.

Soon after that, I am in desperate need of something to drink, but I'm not sure if I should head out into the living room just yet. I open the bathroom door very quietly, expecting the bolt and hinges to emit their creaking sound. I make sure the door opens just a smidgeon through which I can slither my way and tiptoe out into the hallway.

As I get closer to the living room, I don't hear anyone talking, just shuffling around on the hardwood floors. Someone is walking around. I see the table out front, in the middle of the room with the sunlight blessing itself onto the narcotics that light up like a halo. I see dark forms cut in and out on the floor. Making my way closer and closer, trying to peek out into the living room, I am absolutely stunned by the sight.

Sly is still on the couch, but Pablo is kneeling between Sly's legs, his head bopping up and down. Sly's holding a black gun to Pablo's head, whispering, "Yeah bitch, suck that dick…yeah." Other shit was coming out of his mouth too, but too faintly for me to hear.

I stand there mesmerized for I don't know how long, actually watching Pablo get down with another guy. I mean, I knew he was gay and all, but I guess I never actually pictured him sucking another man's dick. I guess you could call it ignorance, or me simply being naive. By any account, it just freaks me out, being high and all. And the gun kind of makes it worse, like one of those porn movies that has a plot so awful you get hooked on it like a soap opera and can't stop watching. I tiptoe back into the bathroom with a strange feeling that I just can't pinpoint. It is something new that I never in my soul ever imagined.

It is really weird!

I sit back down on the toilet, continuing to watch the event in the living room over and over in my head, my hands starting to tremble. My stomach turns into knots. I grab the baggie from out of my blue jeans pocket and snort another line, then another, then another, until it is gone…until I am gone. Then it goes pop. I am not sure if it's my brain exploding as I lay on the smooth texture of the bathroom floor mat, or someone lighting off firecrackers.

Footsteps.

Someone is walking all around the apartment and into the hallway. I hear Pablo's bedroom door open up. I recognize it because it sounds real close. Then, I hear another pop, and another and another.

Then, my bathroom door is slowly nudged open, and in walks Sly laughing with bright gold teeth that make my eyes twitch.

I smile back.

"I think I heard a pop bottle explode," I say, lying on the floor immersed in white light, feeling like I'm lying on a water bed. I grab at the white tiles on the floor, trying to yank them up over my body like a blanket. I think it's time for a nap.

"Fo' real. Ya thirsty kid, cause I gotta another pop bottle fo' ya to drank."

"Cool brotha," I reply, watching a halo form above his head, then turn into flames. He cocks his hand back, leans over me, grabs the back of my head, and smacks the gun right on top of my noggin. Then the stars come out, a lot more than the other night.

The next thing I know I'm lying on a cloud or something.

I hear Anna calling my name from down below the ground, the same time a train is leaving the station.

I look down and see she is resting on a bench a couple feet from the tracks, watching the smoke from the moving train evaporate into the night light. I ask her what she is doing there. She doesn't answer, just keeps calling out my name. First I hear her say, "Solomon." Then, "Sol."

She looks up, so I know she sees me, but as I continue to shout her name really, really loud, she refuses to answer.

I lean over, drawing in a huge breath to scream her name with every confidence she will hear me, but instead I fall off. I just drop down with a cool chill from the sky, still looking up but feeling so melancholy, as that nice quiet spot becomes nothing more than a black void in the sky, getting bigger and bigger. I fall from the sky until I wake up on Pablo's bathroom floor, having no clue what just happened...

CHAPTER 22

❀

Hector's dead. Pablo's dead.

I think I have the gun that did it in my hand. I'm not sure. I just woke up on the bathroom floor with it in my hand.

Now, I'm sitting at the empty dining room table, which was once filled with all types of drugs. Sly must have taken them. I'm looking at Pablo, who's still on his knees. His face is planted on the cushion of the couch, his mouth wide open and eyes looking up to the left.

Blood and brains are on the floor. I immediately throw up, then I bum-rush the whole apartment, looking for anything to lift me off.

That's when I find Hector. I see his feet on the bed, with blood on the curtains. I know eventually I will need to go in there, and look for my lift off, but right now I'm okay with just sitting back at the table and feeding off of adrenaline, looking at the gun that's in my hand and that I think Sly had planted in my hand to pin the rap on me.

I now have a softball-size bump on the top of my head. It starts to throb as the sun beats down. I can feel it pulsating.

I need to get back my wits and figure out what to do first.

Where will I go? I don't know. I will need money. I will need to lift off. I have to speak with Anna. Should I tell her or not? What do I do with the gun? Do I keep it or not? Should I call the cops before I leave?

I get up off of the chair and find a blanket, which I throw over Pablo's dead body, hoping it would make it a little easier for me to float around the room, getting shit done without having to look at him. I collect all my clothes at the corner of the room, stuff them into a duffel bag, and place everything on the table. Then, I go into the kitchen and start going through each cupboard and drawer, hoping to find some dope or hidden money.

I don't make like I'm in a hurry, like you see in the movies when a guy is shuffling through everything and throwing it all around getting desperate when what he's looking for isn't there. I'm pretty calm for the most part, just trying to keep my head together to avoid mistakes. I know the cops will eventually come, and I don't want to be around when they do, so I must hurry.

"Get you head together," I tell myself.

The coffee jar is filled with coke and the sugar bowl with weed.

I go through Pablo's pockets, keeping his head covered so I won't have to look in his eyes, which remind me of Jesus on the crucifix looking up and to the side, feeling the nails in his hands and feet.

Pablo's pockets yield three hundred dollars.

I go to the hallway, where I stop in front of Pablo's room. I don't know if I can bear seeing Hec. But then, I hear sirens from a distance. I have no time to waste. I quickly walk in and look at the wall. I walk to the opposite side of the room, so I don't have to see him, and just go through all the drawers. I find women's thongs and lingerie, dresses, and tight tops.

I take everything that looks of any value in Pablo's jewelry case.

I go through each pair of jeans and find at least a couple bucks in each pocket. Then, as I turn around to walk out, I see Hec lying there face up to the ceiling with a big hole oozing blood on the side of his head. His eyes are closed.

He looks peaceful, probably the only time I've seen Hec like this, besides the morning down at the creek when he was looking up to the sky. I'm not sure how this made me feel, happy that he's now at peace? or angry that someone has dropped the ball on a person I love? He is truly the only friend I have ever loved, maybe even the only person I loved.

Nevertheless, I know that if I ever find that Sly fucker I have to kill him, because that's what Hec would do for me. I am at my last straw. I figure that evil being ever at my side, I'll go out with a bang.

I cover Hec with a blanket and walk out, shutting the door behind me with a couple of tears rolling down my cheeks. I wipe them off and do a bump up my nose before leaving.

Grabbing all my stuff, I tell myself that when I see a pay phone, I'll call the cops and give them the name of the man who did this. Then, I'll call Anna and tell her the bad news. As for me, the only thing I can do is wander to another place.

I feel like I've aged ten years in ten minutes.

My name is Solomon and I'm sixteen years old. My name is Solomon and I've lost hope. My name is Solomon and I have no place to go.

I walk down the dark stairwell and back out into the street, with only one question: What the hell am I gonna do next?

The words scraped on the bathroom stall walls read *Lost-You're fucked-HA HA HA.*

I'm doin' a couple bumps of coke up my nose in the bathroom stall at the train station. I lean against the back of toilet, watching the walls close in and out with every breath I take.

I have the black gun gripped in my hand. I don't know what to do next.

Hec's death is still on my mind. I still can't believe he's dead. My only friend who'd go to war with me if I asked him to, the only one who would jump in with me if I got into some deep water. And now he's dead.

His cousin killed him.

Sly killed him.

I killed him.

I put the gun back in my bag and think about revenge, about killing Sly myself, but I don't have the balls or the anger of ten pissed-off men to go and do that. The city is bigger than me, too big for me to have a straight thought. I feel lost, physically and mentally. For the time being, I can sleep at the train station until the money and drugs run out, but I have no clue what to do after that.

Hector is gone.

Anna's gone, but she wants me to come back.

That's what sticks in my head, after watching Hector over and over again in my head. Someone still wants me around. I don't want to be alone. All I want is to be loved, to find that special someone. I guess what everyone says is right, after all, that I'm too young. But, I wish I didn't have to figure it out this way.

I leave the bathroom stall and walk over to the faucet to throw some water on my face. I look at myself in the mirror and see nothing but bloodshot eyes and a rapidly aging face. A guy in a suit walks in and uses the faucet next to me, looking at himself in the mirror, combing his hair. I look at him and ask if he has any kids. He nods his head yes.

"They're fucked," I utter, then walk out to find a payphone.

CHAPTER 23

❁

"Anna, Hec's dead."

Tears bead down my face. Sniffling, I try to hide my face in the phone booth so no one around sees.

"What," she yells in disbelief.

"Yeah…Some drug dealer came by and killed everyone, Hec and his cousin, then planted the gun in my hand while I was knocked out."

"Oh, my God. Are you okay?" She asks.

"Yeah, I'm fine. I left before the cops came." Then, there's a moment of silence. As a bulge builds up in my throat, I break down crying hard, slurring the words, *What am I gonna do now? I need help!*

"I'm so sorry," she sniffles. "You need to get out of there, Sol. You need to come back home."

"But, I can't," I yell angrily. "The cops are looking for me there."

"I know but, honey, you have no other choice."

She called me, honey. The first time I've heard someone say something sweet to me in a long time.

"But, Anna, I'm scared. I'll be gone for so long."

"Don't worry," she utters softly. "We can do this."

"What do you mean *we*?" I say, wiping the tears from my eyes with my sleeve.

"I…I love you, Sol."

When she whispered those words from the other end the whole station fell silent. My heart starts racing like crazy. It makes me feel so good for a split second that I feel like I'm just on vacation making a long distance call to the one I love, not in the fucked-up state I'm in right now.

Anna's the white beam of light that only comes out when it's pitch black out.

Anna, the angel who cares. Anna, my star that hides behind the building.

"I'll come back," I say shivering.

I look at the board high above to see when the next train is leaving. She says she'll meet me at the station back home to pick me up.

"We'll go back to my house, take a bath and make some food. We'll order a pizza and rent some movies just like senior skip day. Do you remember that Sol?" She says ever so caring and sweet, sniffling in between each word.

"Yeah…It was one of my best days."

"Then, just hide out until your train leaves and come home to me."

A smile breaks from my face. My lips are numb. Don't think just do it, my mind tells me.

"Sol…there's one more thing," Anna says quietly.

"What's that?"

"I'm pregnant," she declares. "I love you…," and hangs up.

My stomach lurches. I hang up the phone and rush over to the front desk to buy my ticket. I decide to buy a magazine and just go back to a bathroom stall and hide out for the next couple hours, until my bus leaves. It's a place I know trouble won't find me.

At the newsstand I grab a book on guns, thinking I can waste some time by learning what all the little knobs do and how a gun actually shoots. I mean I know that the little knob to the right is the safety, and when the red dot is exposed it won't fire, but what the fuck is so safe about that. I once knew a kid who had the shakes all the time back at home. If he had that gun in his hand and the safety was on, it would take just one little shake of the thumb and that thing would be back on again and, hell, I'd be running once that happened.

I walk up to the counter. The man on the other side is leaning his elbows against the cash register watching a little TV screen. I hand him the money and watch, waiting for my change while the game show is stopped and switched to a breaking story. Then, I see Pablo's apartment building with a group of people, some of whom work at the market across the street. I see hookers at the bus stop and people who live in the building standing out front watching as the paramedics and the cops run in and out putting yellow tape all over the place.

The news lady says that there's been a shooting on the fourth floor with two bodies found dead, maybe due to a drug deal gone bad. The camera then goes from outside to inside Pablo's apartment, showing the couch where I used to sleep with a white sheet over it and a big hump in the middle who I expect to be Pablo. The cameraman then walks into the bedroom where another white sheet lies over the bed, red spots soaked through, and Hector is covered.

The news lady is back on camera, telling whoever's watching that the cops have found drugs all over the house and fingerprints that they are dusting right now. She also states that some tenants claim a big black man had parked his car out front and entered the apartment. The little old lady from across the hall told police that he was the only one who walked out.

As the newspaper guy gives me my change, I keep my eye on the TV set. But there's nothing about some short Caucasian with a shaved bleached head entering or leaving. I still feel paranoid, and I start looking over my shoulder as I put the change in my pocket.

The newspaper guy is shaking his head in disgust. Everyone who walks by me flips me out. I can't stop looking around the mobs of people walking back and forth around the train station.

I grab my bag with the magazine and my stuff and walk quickly to the restroom where I know I'll be safe until my bus leaves. My head turns left and right continually. I hope I don't get stopped. Finally, I open the door and run into a stall, shutting it behind me and sitting on the toilet. I feel secure here.

You're fucked!—says the writing on the wall.

CHAPTER 24

❀

If Anna's pregnant like she says she is, how could it be mine? I wore a condom. How do I know she didn't fuck that Calvin kid before me?

Is this a trick? When I get off the train will I be waiting for cops to pick me up instead of Anna?

This is what happens when you start doing mounds of drugs. You don't want to bring any back with you. The problem is that you don't wanna throw them out, either. So you do as much as you can take. That's when you start to get paranoid and start analyzing everything just because you're alone and hiding out.

How the fuck am I gonna take care of a kid?

This is the question I keep asking myself as I flip through the pages of the magazine, paying no attention to their contents. I am just flipping page after page, thinking about Anna's pregnancy and that I might be a dad. Then, I hear a stall door open up.

"Yo kid, you need ta get the fuck outta town, yo."

"All right, man. Damn, just chill out. We'll get my ticket, go back to da crib, pick up some shit and head outta town, aright?"

"Aright, man, just don't take fo'eva, like you usually do."

"Man, jus' shut up and take a piss."

That voice sounds familiar. I think to myself as I slowly close the magazine trying to not make the pages crunch into a loud noise. I try to peep through the crack between the bathroom stall door and the wall, to catch a glimpse of who's taking a piss, but all I see are their backs as they use the stalls.

"So, where ya gonna go till the shit cools down," I hear one say, as he looks over to the side to address the pisser next to him.

"Yo, I gots this girlie in a couple states over who'll let me chill for a little while, ya know. Just some Betty I met awhile back when I went to go visit mom's and shit."

"Fo' real. Is she cute?"

"Man, what you think! All the women I kick it with are bad, ya know what I'm sayin'?"

"Sly, you a sly stone, brotha."

My stomach just drops out of my ass and into the toilet bowl. My eyes are the size and the color of red apples. I feel the hairs on my arms rise as I hear that name Sly a couple feet over. The shock I'm feeling gives me tunnel vision.

He must be on the same schedule as me!

I'm frozen solid with my feet against the stall door. He probably saw the same news report I did on the news, or was informed by one of his goons. Who knows why he's here? All I know is he tried to set me up for killing my best friend. If he knows I'm still out and never got caught, then I'm a dead man for sure.

"Yo, kid, I can't believe that lil' fucker got up after that hit, yo. I know I laid a brotha out, ya know what I'm sayin?"

Well, there goes that idea of trying to hide. Stay calm-they'll leave soon.

"Yo, Sly, all I know is don't worry about that shit cause tha' kid probably knows if he gets caught he'll be fucked too, ya know. So don't worry," I hear his friend say. I peep through the crack again watching him pick his fade in the mirror.

"Aright man, I won't sweat it, but if ya see that muthafucka, pop his ass outta any joint. Ya bust 'im, ya know what I'm sayin'".

"Yo man, bet."

I hear the faucets run. All I can think of is that if I'm seen, I'm fucked. I just have to stay calm. That's what I keep telling myself-remain calm! When people wash their hands, that usually means they're about to leave. Always wash your hands after you piss. If there's a blower use it for a couple of seconds then wipe the rest on your pants. Don't stand there if others want to use it. Public restrooms usually smell bad anyways. This one has that toxic smell of freshly sprayed paint, the kind you inhale to give yourself a high, then get sick to your stomach and make your nose hairs curl up.

I'm starting to feel sick. They're still using the sink. I close my eyes.

In my head, the projector begins to roll-it's a movie of Pablo's apartment. I don't see myself in it, but I'm like a cameraman walking around filming everything. At first, I'm back in the bathroom with a close-up of the white tiles on the wall, then the door opens up and the camera moves down the hall, which is dark but not pitch black dark. Just gray dark, like the sun hiding behind a cloud bleeding a gray mute tone to each color in the apartment.

The camera keeps drawing forward, as the gray becomes a little brighter, and moves closer to the living room. I see the corrugated shadow of a branch that looks twenty feet long as it hits the chair and the table. When I reach the end of the hall the camera turns to the left, exposing the couch, where Sly sits alone, his legs extended, chilling. He doesn't move, but as I get a couple inches closer, in a slow deep bass tone he asks, "What the fuck do you want punk?"

No on answers, but he continues to stare.

"What tha fuck you want?" He says again, like a 45 record playing at 33 1/3 speed.

He gets up slowly off the couch and stands, without moving either forward or back, throwing his hands up yelling, "What, man? What?"

Then, a gun pops up into the screen and begins to fire off in sync with Sly's slow persona. I watch the bullets moving closer and closer.

Sly's eyes grow. He puts his hands up in front of his face. I see the bullets enter his body and his flesh rip open, like a surgeon were cutting up his rib cage. Blood splatters from his back onto the window.

The gray just turned a pinkish red color.

Sly drops to the ground. I feel a smile on my face.

The camera wiggles up and down a few times as if someone were tapping it on the back, and as it turns around, Sly stands there with a big golden smile, his arm above his head and swinging down, like he did to me in the bathroom, causing the camera to fall suddenly to the ground and making my eyes open up. I realize I'm still in the washroom stall, on the toilet scared as fuck.

But this immense anger grows inside me, the same feeling I got when I hit that kid over the head with a bottle. My hands shake wildly, the heat turns up a few notches in my body, and my teeth chatter.

It's kind of peculiar, because it reminds me of Morse code, and I can't even comprehend the code. But for some reason, at this very moment, it's as clear as day. Everything is telling me-H-E-K-I-L-L-E-D-H-E-C-T-O-R-H-E-K-I-L-L-E-D-H-E-C-T-O-R.

Over and over and over again, until I get the balls to drop my feet from the stall, reach into my bag and grab the gun. I drop kick the fucking door until it tears off its hinges and completely opens the space up. Pointing the gun at these guys, I feel as free as a convict would after his release from prison.

Sly's friend turns around quickly when he hears the sound, and pops backwards, throwing his hands up in the air and resting his ass against the sink. But Sly still has his back to me. I think I have a smirk on my face, but I couldn't say for sure.

I yell, "Turn around, you punk," really loud. Sly looks at me through the mirror, dropping his head down and placing his hands on the sink.

"You killed Hec, you piece of shit. You deserve somethin' real bad."

I didn't know what I was gonna do next, but I hear my train is boarding from the intercom outside. I didn't want to kill them, just scare them, and then walk out the bathroom and run to my train at the exact moment it was leaving, so they couldn't catch me.

I stand motionless without saying a word. Sly's boy pleads with me not to shoot him, almost to the point of tears. "Pl-l-lease, ma-a-an, don't shoot me!"

I hear the intercom call my train again. This time I back up into the bathroom while pointing the gun at the back of Sly's head, leaning down very slowly to grab my bag. Feeling the rough fabric of the strap in my palm, I grip it tightly and pick it up to hoist it over my shoulder. Then, I bend back down to grab my magazine, which I think is right next to the bag, but I couldn't feel it on the tiled floor, so I drop my eyes for a split second with the gun pointing at Sly's head. The magazine's halfway between my stall and the next one, so I lean over to grab it then, put my eyes back on Sly, who's now turning around with his hand down his pants. That's when the washroom echoes a huge storm that will pass only when Sly and I run out of bullets.

When it is over, my ears are ringing savagely, as if two alarm clocks were strapped to each one.

I think I hit Sly and his friend a couple of times.

Sly's friend is lying motionless on the ground, blood pouring out of his chest. Sly slides out of the bathroom door. I hear a constant scream from the outside in the station until the door shuts.

My train is announced again over the intercom.

I'm sitting back on the toilet, taking breaths so deep I start to feel lightheaded. I drop the gun to my side and rest my hands on my thighs.

Sly's friend hasn't moved.

I reach over to grab my bag, deciding the best thing I can do right now is get the fuck out and get on that train before it takes off without me.

I can't miss Anna; I'm almost there.

As I reach for the ground, I feel a pressure against my chest that doesn't allow my arm to extend to the ground. I lean back against the toilet and try again, but I can't do it. That's when I see the blood.

Blood soaking through three little holes in my shirt.

My chest begins to pulsate. My head feels cloaked. My ears are clogged up. I try again, this time just to stand up and walk out, forgetting about the bag, but my legs are numb, splattered with blood that I'm not sure I own. I lean back against the toilet and take a couple of deep breaths, but this time they're a lot shorter. I feel my eyes getting heavy. My neck gives out, dropping my head into my chest. My limbs drop to the side. My eyes flicker; I try like hell to keep them open.

I manage to kick the toilet stall door open with my leg. I watch as it swings back and forth, opening then closing, giving me a glimpse of broken sinks that are on the ground, a body drenched in a pool of blood and pieces of mirror shattered across the tile.

The stall stays open and I see myself for the first time, sitting on the toilet, coated with dry blood around my lips and the side of my face from a piece of broken mirror that's right by the left foot of Sly's dead friend.

I don't look good. I can tell from the slanted beady eyes, the darkness of my pupils, the saliva that's hanging from my mouth. I continue to stare at my eyes, remembering that day awhile back when I did coke at my house after leaving Anna's. I recall standing in my bathroom, inhaling bump after bump of coke, staring at myself right after watching my pupils open ever so slightly bigger and bigger after each bump. This time I watch as that broken piece of mirror comes to me. It actually levitates from across the ground and stops mid air right in my face. It focuses on my eyeball. I watch as it grows bigger and bigger in my reflection. Then the mirror itself flies a little above my head and starts to drop down until the mirror shows nothing more than my black pupil and begins to devour me whole like food until I'm back in that dark tunnel, walking towards the light. But, this time I don't ask where I'll be going, I know I've asked many times before and never got an answer. I need to know what's on that other side of my eye. Find out what's hiding in the back of my mind.

The light gets bright, so bright in fact that I have to stick my hand over my face as a shield to protect it from the rays. At this point, I don't know if I should continue. Should I ask now? Should I ask where I'm going? Or should I just walk through?

I decide since I've gotten this far I might as well continue, and I take that first step forward watching my shoe glisten white and yellow as it goes further into the light. I close my eyes and jump through hoping to make at least one good decision in my life.

And as I walk with my eyes closed, still seeing the light emanate bright from the inside of my eye lids, I begin to hear the sound of running water and I feel a breeze hit me from the left. I put my hands out in front of me with my palms down, and feel the tips of tall grass pass back and forth between my fingers. I open my eyes very, very, slowly and see a creek in front of me: The Creek.

The creek that I grew up around.

The creek I played at as a child.

The creek that I jumped across to become a man.

I take a few steps back, deciding to jump across to the other side and go home to my apartment that I can see from here. I begin to run, smiling that I have another opportunity at things before they go sour. I feel joy, believing I have made a worthy decision to continue walking instead of asking where I am going.

If I did ask would I have woken up on the bathroom toilet still dressed in blood? If I asked where I was going, would it be possible that I might wake up next to Hector. If I asked would I be in the hospital or jail from the blood and gunfire in the bathroom?

As my first foot leaves the ground, I feel this happiness to jump across and journey home. My other foot follows and I fly across to the other side, planting both of my feet on the ground, holding my fists and shaking them up and down as if I have just won an Olympic metal. But, as I look up, my apartment complex isn't there anymore. I am at a bus station—a place that looks familiar like I know I've seen it before, but can't put my tongue on it.

"Where have I seen this place before?" I ask myself.

CHAPTER 25

❀

I'm on a train. I'm looking around and discover I'm in a boxcar, sitting on a long sofa, looking out the window as the earth passes by at a tremendous speed.

It's still daytime and I'm in the same old clothes.

I hear thunder. With a loud screech of the brakes, the train slowly makes the earth slow down. The country is visible now instead of one big blur of color. I see the grass that extends for miles until it merges with the ocean of blue from heaven.

I move closer to the window and place my head against the cool glass, looking out and seeing the station not too far ahead. From a distance, I see a couple people standing around, as the brick station gets closer and closer to my car.

It's time to get up and see if Anna's waiting for me. I imagine her brown hair that curls under her chin and her deep dimples when she smiles.

I look out the window and see one soul sitting cross-legged on the bench. Her eyes fixed on the train.

As my train comes to a complete stop I rise from my seat and push the button on the door, waiting for it to open up. I see Anna as she continues to sit, gazing at the train as she waits for me to come out. Her hair glimmers with the sun. I still notice that she still has those soft bouncy curls under her chin. She's in white, a short summer dress sitting alone with her legs crossed.

The door still hasn't opened.

I wave at her, but she doesn't see me. Thinking maybe the windows have an outside tint, I bang on the glass hard so she can hear me.

Her head turns back and forth the length of the train.

The doors refuses to open up.

That's when I hear it, a long drawn out trumpet-like note, telling me the train's about to leave again. Anna gets up from the bench and puts her hand over her forehead to shade her eyes from the bright sun, looking back and forth anxiously waiting for me to get out.

I start to bang on the door with all my might, kicking it, hitting it with my fist, digging my nails into its crevices to pry it open, but still it doesn't open.

"Wait!" I shout, hoping someone hears me. "Wait, this is where I get off!"

But the train slowly moves on, as Anna looks out, waiting for me to get off.

"Wait", I yell out, "Anna! I'm here. This fuckin' thing won't let me out."

I continue to kick and plead, kick and yell. Cry and pray…for this thing to open up, but it just keeps moving, and Anna begins to drift away.

I watch as her hand leaves her forehead and falls on her other arm. Her head drops down and begins to shake as a single tear drops from her head down to the concrete ground.

"N-o-o-o," I yell at the top of my lungs, sliding down to the floor. I feel the momentum of the train as it moves faster and faster down the tracks. I put my knees into my face, cover my legs with my arms, and cry. I wish it would just stop.

But it doesn't.

After a while, when my tears dry up and my nose stops running, I slowly move myself off the floor and hit the button to open the door of the next car over. Walking through the aisle, I see only empty seats. The sun is as bright as ever but everything is eerily quiet.

I hit the button to the next car. There are tables and chairs and curtains on the windows. Walking in, I notice a little old man in a light brown three-piece suit and hat, holding a cane and sitting alone at one of the tables. He is looking out the window.

I walk up to him and ask him, "Where is the next stop at?"

"Oh, I'm afraid there isn't one for quite some time, young man. Should've gotten off sooner," he says in a quiet child-like voice.

"Well, which one is it?" I say, feeling a little confused.

"I'm not too sure myself. The wife used to say how I was always so eager to get off these things, and I should just sit down and enjoy the ride." He says giggling.

"Where are ya goin' then?" I ask.

"I'm not sure about that, either. The last thing I remember, I was lying quietly in a hospital bed. When my eyes shut, I found myself on the train. Kind of peculiar. Would you care to join me?"

I sit down across from him and look out into the fields passing by us.

"You know, I remember the first time I rode on one of these things when I was a child. My mother bought us two tickets to the big city, cause that's where my father worked and we were going out that way to look at houses. I remember she let me have the window seat, because I was pulling on her dress the whole way to the station, bugging her to give it to me. When she finally did, I have to say, that was one of the finest feelings of freedom I ever felt. Even in my old years."

I glance at the old man, still relishing his thought, but then I turn to the window, through which I notice the fields getting brighter and brighter, as we keep going. The grass is swaying back and forth. Loose flower petals are flowing with the rhythm of the train for miles all around and swoop back down into the tall green grass, before popping out as the grass begins to sway in a different direction.

I'm about to say something, I think about how I missed my spot, but before I can speak, the old man stops me. He places his finger over his lips and points to the window, signaling that I should continue to look out.

I do.

The colors of the earth begin to blend together. It's one of the most beautiful things I've ever seen.

I think Anna would enjoy something like this.

I go on watching with only the mute sound of wind.

Anna isn't here with me. Yet, as sad as that sounds, I'm finally at peace.

I continue looking outside, taking a peep here and there at the old man and his smile, deciding that maybe for now I should enjoy whatever I want, not worry about others.

For the first time I feel a relief, a sense of closure with the past. I'm moving forward.

I gaze out at the field of wild flowers. The old man and I are approaching the point where the earth kisses the sky to be free of all the worries from our past. I finally feel released from my anger, and I sit back and enjoy the ride.

About the Author

DeLeon DeMicoli lives in Detroit, MI. He is currently working on his second novel *A Blanket of Sickness*, and a book of short stories called *The Evils of Man*.

0-595-23438-0

Printed in the United States
6142